She awoke to find him in her bed...

Her nightdress had slipped from one shoulder and Jancis saw Thorp's dazed look rest there before his eyes finally met hers. It was as plain as day that Thorp had no recollection of how he came to be in her bed—he was of the opinion that he had been welcomed! The idea made her furious. Tearing her eyes from his face, she turned to bury her head in the pillow.

"How could you?" she demanded accusingly. There was a dumbfounded silence, as she had expected.

"You don't even remember, do you?" she moaned. "You were too drunk to remember."

"Are you trying to tell me that in a drunken state I came to your room and made love to you?" he finally demanded. "That I *seduced* you?"

"Thorp," she said painfully, "what if I'm pregnant?"

Books by Jessica Steele

HARLEQUIN PRESENTS

HARLEQUIN ROMANCES

These books may be available at your local bookseller.

For a list of all titles currently available,
send your name and address to:

Harlequin Reader Service
P.O. Box 52040, Phoenix, AZ 85072-2040
Canadian address: P.O. Box 2800, Postal Station A,
5170 Yonge St., Willowdale, Ont. M2N 5T5

JESSICA STEELE

gallant antagonist

Harlequin Books

TORONTO • NEW YORK • LONDON
AMSTERDAM • PARIS • SYDNEY • HAMBURG
STOCKHOLM • ATHENS • TOKYO • MILAN

Harlequin Presents first edition September 1984
ISBN 0-373-10725-0

Original hardcover edition published in 1981
by Mills & Boon Limited

CHAPTER ONE

THE most important thing Jancis Langfield had on her mind that Saturday afternoon was whether or not she wanted to go to the party she had been invited to that night. William, her brother, had left the flat they shared only that morning to join an archaeological expedition in Northern Greece, and already she was missing him, for all he had grown into a quiet young man.

A year older than herself, he hadn't always been like that, she reflected. A grin of remembrance crossed her face as she recalled the madcap things the four of them had got up to in the old days. Sophie, the youngest of the group, had always been the ringleader. It was amazing now to think of the mischief she had thought to get them all into, for like sheep they had all followed.

She had kept in touch with Sophie, though she hadn't seen anything of her for a few months. Sophie hadn't changed at all then and Jancis thought that since her mischief-drawn friend was now twenty-one, there was very little likelihood she was going to. Of Davy, the fourth in their quartet, she had seen nothing for over twelve months now. Not since that day he had dropped in at the flat with his artist's easel and rucksack, cadged a bed for the night, then with the easiness of old friends departed the next day with a casual, 'See you!'

Jancis' mind drifted on to the party she had been invited to. Should she go? It would take the rawness away of knowing it could be months or years, depending how the dig went, before she saw her brother again. He had been away before, of course; he had needed to gain experience before they would even consider him for this expedition. As it was, he had been of the opinion that as

5

he was so junior his role would be that of tea-maker-in-chief. But this time she had a feeling that with his foot firmly on the first rung of the archaeological ladder, the times he returned to the London-based flat would be few and far between.

Did she want to go to Primrose Zollman's party, though? The last two or three parties she had been to hadn't been exactly boring, but when she arrived home from the last one William had still been up and had been surprised to see her, exclaiming, 'You're home early!' It had dawned on her when his remark had flitted through her mind the next morning that at one time she had so enjoyed being one of the body-gyrating, every-word-a-wisecrack crowd, she had now changed from being one of the last to leave to being one of the first.

Perhaps I'm getting old, she thought, going into the kitchen to fix herself something to eat. She had had a birthday yesterday. Twenty-three and never been kissed. And that was a lie, she thought without humour, remembering those hectic moments with Shaw. Quickly she turned her thoughts away from Shaw. It still hurt.

Perhaps she had outgrown going to the type of party she had always so enjoyed? Her mind drifted over the people who would probably be there tonight. And then, simply, her decision was made. Primrose was bound to have invited Adrian Hayward, and since she was sure he would ask, have been told that she had been invited too.

Adrian was becoming too much, Jancis decided. She knew he was in love with her, and remembering her own hurt over Shaw she had tried to let him down gently. But he was very persistent, was Adrian. 'I'll make you love me,' he had declared, having no idea her heart was dead.

Rapidly going off the idea of food, she went to stand at the door of William's room. Neat and tidy, everything in its place. He had even made his bed, she saw. Going into his room, she pulled back the top cover intending to strip it, when the phone in the sitting room shrilled.

Unhurriedly she let the cover drop from her hands and returned to the sitting room, her mind going over several people who could be calling.

'Jancy?' queried a voice she had no trouble in recognising. Sophie! She was one of the very few people who shortened her name that way.

'Hello, Sophie,' said Jancis, her voice welcoming. Life was never dull when Sophie was around. 'I've just finished thinking about you and here you are. How . . .'

'I'm ringing to say many happies for yesterday. Sorry I'm a bit late,' Sophie gabbled. 'I would have rung you yesterday, but I've been having a bit of trouble with the parents.'

Typical Sophie, Jancis thought, feeling better already. Other parents had trouble with their children, but Sophie would have to be different.

'What have you been up to now?' she questioned, knowing without a doubt that 'parent trouble' for Sophie meant she had been caught out in a misdemeanour of some sort. 'Or shouldn't I ask?'

'Nothing, honestly.' Sophie brought out her stock phrase that had Jancis' lips twitching. 'I've been so good lately you just wouldn't believe.' She didn't believe it, but didn't say so. 'Actually,' Sophie said slowly after a moment, 'I'm a bit bored at present, and was passing the hall table and saw your birthday present lying there——' she broke off to insert a petulant, 'Wouldn't you think somebody would have seen it lying there and popped it in the post for me? However,' she went on brightly, 'seeing it there reminded me I hadn't rung you and I thought, I know, I'll deliver it personally.'

A bored Sophie meant trouble with a capital T. 'I'd love to see you,' said Jancis, her affection for her friend overcoming any qualms she might have about Sophie's disrupting influence. She then explained about William having gone off that morning, and it was all Sophie needed to promptly invite herself to stay.

'I can have his room, then. I'll be no trouble, honestly,' and just in case her friend needed a bribe, 'I can cook now,' she stated proudly.

Jancis laughed out loud. Sophie's idea of cooking was most likely tinned spaghetti on toast. 'I think I'll be able to manage to cook for the two of us,' she told her, having kept house for her and William for the past five years. 'When are you coming?'

'I'll start now,' said Sophie promptly, giving Jancis the definite impression that she already had her weekend case packed. 'Er—any life going on down there at the moment?' she thought to ask, and knowing Sophie wouldn't be content to stay in that night, Jancis found herself telling her:

'Well, there is this party tonight, but . . .'

'Super,' replied Sophie, who had no inhibitions about going where she hadn't been invited. 'I'm on my way!'

Jancis put down the phone, collected fresh bedlinen, then returned to William's room to remake the bed, thinking it wouldn't take Sophie very long to get here from Buckinghamshire in her nippy little sports car.

The bed made, she collected one or two ornaments from her own room to soften the effects of the plainness William preferred, then took one of the two vases of flowers from the sitting room and placed them on the chest in the bedroom Sophie was to use. After that she pottered about in the kitchen, fixing a couple of plates of ham salad. Sophie had a trim, slim figure like herself, but had told her the last time she had seen her that she was dieting. There was time, then, to take a few deep and relaxing breaths which she knew would be the last she would draw until the weekend was over and Sophie had waved goodbye. Half an hour later a ring at the door announced her friend's arrival. The smile on Jancis' face was warm and genuine as she went to let her in.

'Sophie!' she beamed when she saw the slender blonde standing there. 'Come in,' she welcomed her, opening the door wide.

Her smile dipped somewhat as she looked towards Sophie's feet, intending to pick up her case. For instead of the small weekend case she had anticipated, at Sophie's feet were two very large travelling cases, plus a weekend case and vanity box.

'I can never make up my mind what to wear,' said Sophie, her blue eyes staring innocently into the clear green eyes of her friend.

'So you brought the lot.'

Sophie grinned infectiously in reply, and between them they carried her luggage to the room she was to use. 'I love this flat,' she opined, kicking off her shoes and trailing into the sitting room behind Jancis. 'You're so lucky being able to live without your parents breathing down your neck.'

The ready smile Jancis had for Sophie faded briefly from her face. She had thought Sophie would have realised that it hadn't been convenient for her father to have her and William with him. It had been his suggestion when they had moved from Little Bramington that at eighteen and nineteen, as she and William had been then, it was about time the apron strings were cut. His suggestion that he bought two flats, one for his occupation and one for theirs. He was a real smoothie, was their father. William hadn't seen the suggestion for what it was, hadn't seen it would cramp Tarquin Langfield's style to have a grown up son and daughter under his roof when he brought home his various women.

'Have I said the wrong thing?' Sophie asked, seeing the change in her face and not hesitating to ask. Then, quick apology in her eyes, 'I'm sorry, Jancy. Does it still hurt that your parents are divorced?'

'No,' said Jancis, forcing a smile. 'It did at the time, as you know. I hated that Father sold the house and we all had to move from Little Bramington as though we were lepers or something.'

Sophie plonked herself gracefully down in one of the chairs, and Jancis followed suit. 'Well, your mother had pricked his pride with a vengeance, hadn't she?' said Sophie, feeling since Jancis had said it no longer hurt, she had carte blanche to bring it out into the open.

'You know all about it?' Jancis asked. 'Oh, I know my father's name is forever in the papers, he can't sneeze if he happens to have some lovely on his arm without it being reported, but you were only about sixteen then, weren't you? When it happened, I mean.'

'I don't think I was ever a dumb blonde,' said Sophie seriously. 'And since I was forever creeping into places where I wasn't supposed to be I heard no end of things that weren't meant for my ears.' Quite unashamedly she told a half admiring, half scandalised Jancis, 'The night it became general knowledge that your folks were splitting, the parents had some people in to dinner—you know, long white tablecloth, the candelabrum bit, the lot. Anyway, I remember I was feeling dead anti because the parents had said I couldn't join them, so I went and camped under the dining room table. I was on the point of dropping off, the conversation was so boring. Then your father's name came up and I pricked up my ears, intending to tell you about it the next day. Only I don't think I did, because they were saying the laugh was on him—how he'd been known as the local Don Juan—his affairs were numerous, apparently—but how your mother had made him a laughing stock because she'd been having a discreet affair with Barney Tavistock almost since the day he moved into the mansion at Fellows Top two years ago, and that now you and William were of age, she'd gone off with him.'

Loyalty to both her parents had Jancis incapable of saying anything against either one of them when Sophie had finished. But that loyalty couldn't have her arguing that what Sophie had overheard was wrong, because it was pretty much what had happened. Though Sophie had left out that her mother had married Barney Tavistock after the divorce and was now living with him in Zurich.

Over their meal Sophie brought her up to date on what was happening in the village they had both been reared in. 'They might as well bury it, it's so dead,' was her opinion before she left the table and went to attend to her unpacking.

Busy with the washing up, Jancis reflected over her parents' marriage. She hadn't thought about it for some time. Sophie's reminder had jerked so many painful memories to life; finding her mother in tears at the age of eleven, discovering at fourteen why her mother cried so often, why at other times she was tight-lipped and refused to talk to her father. At first she had thought the atmosphere in the house was all her mother's fault, and hadn't been able to understand why she should so constantly be nasty to him the whole time.

That was until shortly after her fourteenth birthday. It had been a Saturday. William and Davy had gone to spend the weekend under canvas a few miles up the road and she and Sophie were going to go on their bikes to see how they were getting on. But she hadn't made it as far as the Ellingtons' house to call for Sophie, because she had fainted and come off her bike. Except for a grazed knee she hadn't hurt herself too badly, but, still feeling peculiar, she had wheeled her bike back home.

Her father, a well known industrialist, often went away for a few days on business. He had gone away the day before, so she had been surprised to see his car standing on the drive. She never had asked why he had come home that day, though in later years she had formed her own opinions as to why he worked weekends when most other girls' fathers were at home.

She had felt better for seeing his car there and had gone into the house to ask him or her mother to look at her knee. But her knee had been forgotten, for as she walked into the hall her ears had been assaulted by the row that was going on in the living room. Never would she forget hearing her mother, shrieking in a voice she had never heard from her before, accusing her father of his latest affair. Like some wound-up tigress, she hadn't stopped there but had gone on to accuse him of numerous other affairs. Shocked, Jancis had stood rooted and heard the accused trying to talk himself out of it. Not believing what she was hearing, she heard her mother saying he could bluster all he liked, that she had the evidence of a private detective. Then finally, when she thought she was going to disgrace herself and be sick on the spot, she heard her father, no longer blustering, but his voice taunting, 'Well, what are you going to do about it? You won't leave me—I know that. You're too goody-goody to be true.'

Jancis hadn't been sick, instead she had fainted again. She had slowly surfaced to find the solidity of the sofa beneath her, and had heard her mother's voice, quiet now, refined, as it always was, saying, 'You'd better go. I don't want her breathing the same air as you any more than she has to.'

Her dizzy and fainting attacks had gone on for about six months. Nothing seriously wrong, the doctor had said, some girls were prone to fainting in the process of growing. She had outgrown the fainting attacks, but not until last year when she had met Shaw had she outgrown the conviction that she never wanted to marry. Up until then she had been convinced she would stay single, would never fall in love; would never love someone so much as to want to marry him, and risk having that marriage turning into a screaming match filled with the mutual loathing she had heard that day.

When Shaw had come into her life she had realised that her crackpot belief that she would never marry was just exactly that. She would marry Shaw like a shot when he asked her. Some marriages—a few, she adjusted her thinking—might be like that of her parents. But not hers. Her marriage to Shaw would be nothing like her parents'. Shaw would be faithful to her as she would be faithful to him. She just couldn't think of it any other way. Fidelity she prized above all things.

But Shaw hadn't asked her to marry him—to sleep with him, to be his mistress, yes, but not to marry him. She hadn't slept with him, but that wasn't because she hadn't wanted to—she had. What had held her back even now she didn't know, for several times it had taken all her will power, plus, to drag herself out of his arms, to say, 'Sorry, darling.'

Her high ideals on fidelity received a near mortal blow when she discovered, through a 'kind friend', that what Shaw wasn't getting from her he was getting from someone else.

She had been disbelieving, completely stunned. She had challenged him about it, only to be even more stunned, since only the day before he had been swearing undying love for her, to hear him admit it. 'I never told you I'd take a vow of celibacy until such time as I could get you to come across,' he told her crudely. Jancis had felt her face drain of colour as she had stared at him, the knowledge growing that all she had been to him was a challenge. Apparently she was the only girl in his little black book without an asterisk by her name. She knew then that as soon as that asterisk had been written in, Shaw Pengelly would continue to date her only until the next new name went into his book.

That 'friendship' had ended last May. It was now January, and although her ideas about never getting married might have changed, her ideals of fidelity in marriage were even more firmly entrenched. She might well get married one day, though she couldn't see it just then, but only when she was two hundred per cent certain that the man she felt she could love for life, felt the same way as she did about that commitment.

'You'll have to get a maid, Jancy,' said Sophie from the doorway. 'I never knew unpacking was such tedious work. I shall instruct the parents to increase Joyce's salary.'

Jancis came back to the present, really glad to have Sophie and her bubbling humour with her. Though had it not been for her open chatter about her parents, she doubted she would have dragged out those painful memories from the recesses of her mind.

'Is Joyce still with you?' she asked, remembering that the Ellingtons' maid had been with them since she could remember.

'Mmm,' Sophie confirmed, her face engagingly alight. 'Can't think why, but she seems to like us. Can I have the bathroom first?'

It had gone eight when they were ready to leave for the party, Sophie looking lovely in a black catsuit, cut daringly low, Jancis thought, and bewailing that she thought she had a spot coming, which she hadn't.

'You look lovely and you know it,' said Jancis.

'You don't look so bad yourself,' Sophie understated, eyeing her friend's titian-haired beauty enviously. 'You're more covered up than me,' she added, admiring the loose-fitting dress of two-tone green that Jancis was wearing, 'yet you still have more . . .' Unable to find the word she wanted, she grinned and tacked on, 'Promise you'll stand in a dark corner and give me a chance to make their eyes pop out.'

'Come on,' Jancis laughed.

They went in Sophie's car. 'You can always drive it

back if I click,' she told Jancis wickedly, and they were both laughing as she carried on in this vein, when they pulled up half an hour later at Primrose Zollman's house.

Jancis didn't have to go looking for her hostess, because it was Primrose herself who came to the door, and rather than looking put out to see an extra guest standing on the dootstep, she appeared delighted. 'Oh, good,' she smiled, when Jancis had made the introduction, explaining that Sophie was staying with her. 'We seem to have a surplus of men at the moment. It won't last, but let me have your cloaks while you go in and even the numbers up a bit.'

Sophie was an instant success, as Jancis had suspected she would be. When it came to dancing, neither girl lacked for partners, though Sophie seemed more than happy to be dancing with the partner she had at the moment than Jancis herself was.

The party was turning out to be much as she had expected it to. I must be getting old, she thought again, finding nothing stimulating in trying to avoid the hands of Vance Kettering who fancied himself as a ladykiller. She danced out of his reach, the ankle length of her dress swirling. Her back to him, she glanced at the door and saw Adrian Hayward had just come in. Oh, grief, she thought, the good humour with which she had arrived at the party having been gradually worn away, he had spotted her and was looking at her with that soulful expression she didn't like. She just didn't feel up to dealing with Adrian's protestations of love tonight. She felt Vance Kettering's hands take hold of her and pull her round towards him. What the hell, she thought, suddenly fed up, the half formed idea growing in her mind that if Adrian saw her responding to someone else, perhaps then he would get the idea that there was no chance for him.

'A bit hot in here, isn't it?' Vance queried.

Oh, crumbs, she thought, didn't he have a better line than that to get her out of this mêlée and alone somewhere? 'Do you think so?' she said calmly, ignoring the suggestion in his voice. 'I thought it just about right myself.'

Vance grinned, his arms coming around her waist regardless that the tape deck was spilling out a beat number and his hold on her was not strictly necessary. If he says, 'You and I could make sweet music together,' I'll thump him, she thought, but mindful that Adrian would still be watching them, she smiled back at her partner.

As he saw her smile, the hold Vance had on her tightened. About to give him a push that would put some daylight between their two bodies, she looked to where Adrian was standing—he was still looking.

She forced herself to relax, so the movement to push Vance away didn't happen, and further encouraged, he planted a kiss on her neck. Gritting her teeth not to give way to revulsion that had her wanting to stiffen in his arms, she again flicked a glance to the door, and immediately felt a bitch that from the stricken look on Adrian's face he thought she was a happy participant in what was going on. Her heart softened towards him; she couldn't be this cruel. About to tell Vance to cut it out, she glanced from Adrian to catch sight of the tall man standing behind him—and there her intention to tell Vance he was playing a solo game went completely from her mind.

Hastily she looked away from the newcomer. Heavens, what a look he had given her! Never had she seen such contempt on anyone's face. And it was all for her! He must be thinking the same as Adrian, must have witnessed Vance Kettering trying to make love to her while they were dancing. She had meant it to look as though she was enjoying it, and had succeeded, if that scorning look was anything to go by. But what did he think it had to do with him? Who did he think he was, anyway, to look at her as though she had just crawled out of the woodwork?

Vance Kettering's hands roving over her back made her aware she had better cool the situation right now. But the stranger's look had affected her more than she thought, and to her own surprise she heard her voice sounding unaccountably husky as she said:

'I—er—don't want to dance any more.'

His eyes lit up, and she forgot about the stranger as she realised the sudden husky tone of her voice had given Vance the impression he had aroused within her the urge to merge. God, she thought in disgust, some men! She'd had this party up to here.

In a mind to find Sophie, who frustratingly seemed to have disappeared, Jancis was all set to ask her if she would mind finishing out the party without her. Sophie had been fully accepted by the crowd and wouldn't mind a bit, she knew, if she wasn't ready to leave yet.

Breaking out of Vance's hold, she gave him a smile she hoped he would read, as 'Sorry, find somebody else,' and left him. The man who had given her that derisory look was still by the door, but was no longer looking at her, his eyes more intent on scanning over the other women in the room. Another stag out hunting, Jancis thought sourly, though secretly she thought the women here were a mite too young for him. He looked to be in his middle thirties, and though not good-looking, he certainly had something about him that could mean he, like Shaw, didn't live the life of a monk. Damn Shaw, she thought, strangely, feeling better about him than she had in a long while.

'Hello, Jancis,' said Adrian as she drew level with him.

About to tell him she was going home, she realised that would leave her wide open to an invitation for him to drive her, since knowing Adrian he would have noted that her car wasn't parked outside.

'Hello,' she answered, and when it looked as though he was going to ask her to dance, 'Bathroom,' she mouthed, letting him think she would be back.

The tall man next to Adrian would have to move if she was to get by him without having bodily contact. 'Excuse me,' she said, when not only had he not looked at her, though he must know she was there, but seemed intent on ignoring her. I'm obviously not his type, she thought whimsically, then felt the full icy blast of the coldest grey eyes as her 'Excuse me' interrupted his search for a female more to his taste.

I know him from somewhere, she thought, feeling shaken that any man, known or unknown, could look at her with such cold dislike. There was no recognition in his gaze as he continued to hold her wide green eyes in that cold hard stare.

'I'd like to get by,' she said huskily, her voice again affected by this cold, uncompromising man.

He stepped out of the way. Jancis thought she caught the words, 'Have a good time,' though she couldn't be sure. Not understanding the remark, though in no mind to turn around and ask him what he meant, she headed for the stairs.

Away from the hard look of him, the sensation that she had met him somewhere before disappeared. She couldn't remember having been introduced to him anywhere. Her memory playing a trick on her, she decided, then went along the landing to check that Sophie wasn't in the bathroom. The bathroom was empty.

Oh well, she'd get her cloak while she was up here and explain to Sophie that she was leaving when she went downstairs again. Only she hoped that man wasn't standing in the doorway when she went down. For while waiting to get by him, even before he had looked down at her as if he had seen better things on a rubbish tip, she had felt a rising antagonism, and didn't trust herself not to push rudely past him rather than politely ask him if she could get by a second time.

CHAPTER TWO

HEADING for the bedroom she thought was the one she had collected her cloak from the last time she had attended one of Primrose's parties, Jancis opened a door to the left of the landing, and fumbled for the light switch.

Light flooded the room, but there were no coats to be seen cluttering up the bed. Oh well, she'd try another door. Backing out of the room, she came up against something solid. She stilled, an apology on her lips, but her apology was never uttered. What did leave her lips was a yelp of surprise as arms came either side of her waist and Vance Kettering's voice murmured in her ear:

'Sorry to keep you waiting. Didn't want to make it look too obvious.'

About to reply with some sharp comment, Jancis half turned and saw he was deadly serious; the look in his eyes telling her exactly what he had in mind.

'Now just a . . .' That was all she had time for. Eager to get her into the bedroom, Vance pushed her forward, waited only to check that the room was empty, then flicked the room into darkness while at the same time closing the door behind him.

Quickly she put some space between them. The room was pitch black, but she knew he was still by the door, so she wasn't ready yet to go anywhere near it to make her departure. Vance was strongly built, and although fairly confident she could get through to him that his idea of fun was not hers, she didn't think that to put herself within reach of his arms would cool his ardour any.

'Are you over by the bed, Jancis?' His voice came softly;

he too was having difficulty in the dark.

She moved to the bed, intending to say, 'Yes', wait for him to move and then dart to the door. Fleetingly the thought of how Sophie would laugh when she related this episode to her passed through her mind. It seemed ages since she herself had got into a scrape, though Sophie was no stranger to them.

'Yes, I'm by the bed,' she whispered back, tensing her muscles ready for flight.

She heard him move, waited her chance, then just as she was about to go into action, had indeed taken one fleeing step, she cannoned straight up against him. 'Oh!' she yelled, more in surprise than fright. Stupid really to have expected him to go to the other side of the bed. 'Let me go, Vance! I didn't . . .' He had her in a bear hug. 'I don't . . .'

Alarm sped through her, her breath going completely as he dragged her on to the bed. No time now to worry that the skirt of her dress had ridden up during the process, Vance was beside her on the bed and by the feel of it as her hand pushed and felt the naked skin of his chest, he had taken off his shirt.

Praying to God that that was all he had disposed of, she went to grab his hair, to pull his seeking mouth away from hers. Then suddenly she froze, then relief surged through her as light flooded the room.

Vance had frozen too. Neither of them had heard the door open. His hold on her slackened, and, about to leap off the bed tossing a few short sharp remarks to him over her shoulder, Jancis looked towards the door and saw the man who had come in and was looking at both of them as if they were a nasty smell was the man who had given her such a hard icy look downstairs when she had asked him to let her by.

Only now did the words he had thrown after her begin to take on any meaning. His instruction to 'Have a good time' was clearly obvious now. He had seen Vance Kettering kissing her while they were dancing and had thought they had come up here on purpose to carry out the intention that had been in Vance's mind, but never in hers.

'This room's taken,' she heard Vance say before she had sufficient saliva to utter a word. Then as a protest rose to her lips, the light went out, and so, unspeaking, did the intruder.

Galvanised into action, the shock at what had happened having to take a back seat while she dealt with a more immediate crisis, Jancis took advantage of her would-be seducer having to find his place, and was off the bed before he knew she had moved. Inwardly she was squirming at the look that man had given her as she leapt to the door. With her hand on the door handle she paused, intending to give Vance the sharp edge of her tongue, then she wondered briefly just how much encouragement she had given him in her efforts to make Adrian see she didn't feel like that about him. Without saying a word she opened the door and stepped out on to the landing.

No longer thinking it a fine tale to relate to Sophie—the party was over as far as she was concerned—Jancis cautiously investigated the other bedrooms until she found the one where the bed was festooned with outdoor wear. Without too much trouble she found her own cloak and was just lifting it from the pile, when a sound in the empty room alerted her to the fact that she was not alone.

It came again. Bed-springs! Funny—there was no one on the bed. Cautiously she lifted the covers that had draped to the floor, lapping them right back. She peered down, and with a sense of amazement saw the blonde head of her friend Sophie.

'Sophie!' she exclaimed, dreading what her friend had got up to now. 'What are you . . . Is there anyone under there with you?'

'Would that there were,' said the irrepressible Sophie, not showing any signs of wanting to come out. Then belatedly, her face going solemn, she hissed urgently, 'How about you—Is there anybody with you?'

'I'm alone,' Jancis told her, wondering if one of the male revellers had frightened her and if she was beneath the bed in hiding. Her brow wrinkled. That wasn't like Sophie. She had seen her come out laughing from situations that would have left her in a trauma for a week.

'What are you up to, Sophie?' she asked severely, feeling responsible for her if she was up to some prank in her friend's house.

Sophie looked thoughtful for a moment, as though in two minds whether to tell her or not. Then, Jancis' loyalty never being in question, she said, 'Well, since I need your help, I suppose I'd better confess.'

She then proceeded to enlighten her stunned friend into the reason why she had found it necessary to bring so much luggage with her when Jancis had thought her visit was for only the weekend. Apparently Sophie was hoping to stay with her for much longer—though only for a month, if she didn't mind.

'It's all the parents' fault,' Sophie complained, her head slowly emerging, though her body was nowhere near ready to follow suit. 'Dad has been overdoing it a bit and Mummy talked him into taking a cruise. I thought it a great idea too,' she added, and Jancis could just imagine the wild time her young friend would have without her parents there to supervise her. 'Then just because I happened to have a party that got a bit out of hand the last time they went away—all that fuss because one of the rooms had to be redecorated, I ask you!—they said I'd have to go and stay with Mummy's brother while they were away.'

She still hadn't got a clue what all this had to do with Sophie hiding beneath the bed, even less what help Sophie

wanted from her. It went without saying that she was
welcome to stay with her while her parents were away,
even if she did visualise the next month being more than
a little hairy.

'But your mother's brother didn't want you to stay with
him,' she guessed, imagining some set-in-his-ways
gentleman holding up his hands in horror at the prospect
of having Sophie landed on him.

'That's right, he didn't,' agreed Sophie. 'Though for
my mother's sake, he said he'd put up with me, only would
they please hurry back.'

'Oh,' said Jancis, wondering if the fog would ever clear,
and guessing again, 'So you told him you'd rather stay
with me.'

'Not exactly,' said Sophie, then, gabbling, 'Mother was
being very uptight about it and Dad was threatening to
cut off my allowance if I refused to go. The only other
alternative being offered was that they'd take me on the
cruise with them. Can you imagine?' she said, horrified.
'I stopped going on holiday with them when I was seven-
teen. I'd be stifled on a cruise ship with their watchful
eyes on me every minute and nowhere to escape to.'

Light was beginning to come through for Jancis. Her
father Sophie had been known to manipulate, her mother
was a much tougher proposition. So it was either join
them on the cruise or go where, in the absence of her
mother's supervision, Mrs Ellington's probably even more
stern brother would be able to keep an eye on her.

'Honestly, Jancy, I'd just die of boredom if I have to
go to my uncle's place. It's miles from anywhere and he'll
be working all hours God sends, so I'll only have myself
for company.' Sophie broke off to exclaim crossly, 'It isn't
even as if he has to work, because he came in for most of
Grandfather's massive fortune. But he spends day after
day shut away in the laboratory he's had built to the side
of his house messing with his test tubes and things, and if

I blot my copybook just once, I know he'll tell my mother, and Dad will do as he's threatened and cut off my allowance. I don't get enough to go round as it is,' she mourned.

Jancis allowed herself a small smile which she hurriedly concealed. Sophie was prone to exaggeration and, up to a few months ago, to her knowledge received a very generous allowance from her father. Her mind lingered on what else Sophie had said.

'Test tubes?' she queried, going off the real subject matter for a moment and thinking this was the most abnormal conversation she'd had to date, given that Sophie's head protruded only very slightly from the bed, while she herself had opted to sit on the floor where she could see Sophie better. Still, what *was* normal while Sophie was around?

'He's an agricultural scientist or something,' Sophie explained. 'Fiddles about with dirt all day to see what crops will grow from soil from various parts of the world.'

Jancis fully saw that the work Sophie's uncle was doing might be in a very worthwhile cause if the end result was that famine-threatened countries were able to grow sufficient quantities of food to keep famine at bay, but she saw too that to have to stay with some crusty old boffin for a month would drive Sophie up the wall. But she was still no nearer to finding out what Sophie was doing hiding under the bed.

'So you didn't tell your uncle you were coming to stay with me. Won't he be expecting you?'

'He *was*,' Sophie confessed. 'I was supposed to drive down to his place in the Cotswolds this afternoon.'

'This afternoon? But . . .'

'But I came to you instead,' Sophie finished for her impishly.

'You telephoned him and told him not to expect you?'

Jancis suggested, and as Sophie slowly moved her head from side to side, 'You didn't telephone him and tell him not to expect you?'

'I didn't.'

'Oh, Sophie! Not only will he be anxious about you, he'll be furious when he knows you've done a flit.'

'I know,' said Sophie, all humour suddenly disappearing from her face.

'He'll have every justification for murdering you when he next sees you,' said Jancis, trying to sound stern, but torn between the desire to laugh and the urge to try and instil in Sophie some sense of responsibility.

'He almost did see me,' Sophie said quietly, then, her sense of humour getting the better of her, 'What do you think I'm doing stuck under this bed?'

'*What!*' Disbelievingly, Jancis stared at her. 'You mean, *he's here?*' Then, knowing she must be mistaken, 'He can't be. How could he? You didn't know you were going to be here yourself until you arrived at my place.'

'He's here,' said Sophie with conviction. 'Don't ask me how he knew where to find me, because I haven't a clue. But I was just on my way downstairs after visiting the loo when I heard some late arrivals at the door. I just couldn't believe my eyes when I saw Thorp. Beating a hasty retreat wasn't in it. Fortunately he didn't see me, though he must have seen and recognised my car outside.'

'Oh,' said Jancis, and suddenly the breath seemed to leave her body.

How could she have forgotten? she thought shaken. The way Sophie had spoken she had been imagining some white-haired man, round-shouldered with specs perched on the end of his nose. But, as the floodgates of her memory unlocked, she knew he wasn't old at all. Sophie had said he was here tonight, and she was right. She had seen him herself—twice; once downstairs and once when he had come into the bedroom where it had looked as though Vance Kettering was making love to her. Her instinct downstairs that told her she knew him hadn't been false either. She did know him. Once before she had met Sophie's uncle, and it seemed impossible now that the years had washed that meeting from her mind. For she had been twelve years old then and had sworn to hate him for the rest of her life. His face then had been seen at first through a blur of fear, before raging fury had ousted it. But to have forgotten that . . .

'I can't go with him,' Sophie wailed, 'I just can't, Jancy! How the blazes he tracked me down I don't know, but since he's one of those sincere types—my word is my bond printed all the way through him—I just know he's got no intention of going back to the Cotswolds without me.'

Jancis began to feel troubled on her behalf. She had been wrong to agree to go and stay with him in the first place and then skip without letting him know. But really, she just couldn't see Sophie sticking it out with that awful cold man until her parents came home.

'I'll come and see him with you . . .' she began, feeling brave in the face of Sophie's panic, thinking to ask him to let Sophie stay with her. Then she realised that would do no good at all. Thorp—what his other name was she couldn't remember, if she ever knew it—had seen her on that bed with Vance. He must have been looking for Sophie, she saw that now. But from his angle it would appear she had been having a fine old time with Vance, and with Sophie's uncle having given his word to take charge of his niece, she just couldn't see him letting go that guardianship to the type of girl he thought she was. 'It wouldn't work, would it?' she tacked on lamely.

Sophie had been thinking. 'I tell you what might work,' she said, having a more devious mind than Jancis. 'It would mean you having to leave the party early, though.'

'I'd just come up for my cloak, actually,' Jancis

informed her, hoping the plan Sophie was about to reveal didn't involve anything too wild; she had never shinned down a drainpipe in her life. 'I've been looking for you to tell you I was going and to give you the spare key to my flat.'

'Great,' said Sophie, full of enthusiasm.

It was the first time Jancis could remember leaving a party without saying goodbye to her hostess. The first time she had made such a racket driving a car away from the kerb, at that time of night too, she reflected, as she drove Sophie's Morgan away from the party.

Following instructions she had made the throttle roar, had ground the gears painfully, noisily, and had the tyres spinning and screeching in protest. Even so, she was doubtful that Thorp Kingman, as she now knew him, would have heard the racket she made. Though as Sophie had pointed out, the tape deck wasn't blaring away *all* the time, and with the hope of a lull in the conversation or neighbours coming to complain about the din, the revving of the car's engine being the last straw, someone might come out to investigate and see that the Morgan, which had been spoken of at some length by the sports car enthusiasts, was no longer there.

Sophie had thought it best if she stayed behind so that in the event of luck going against them, should Thorp chase after the Morgan, then he would not find Sophie the driver, but an innocent-looking Jancis who was to say Sophie had called to see her that afternoon and had lent her her car for a few days. Sophie often lent her car out, apparently.

She slowed her pace as the car neared her flat, a look in her rear view mirror assuring her that she wasn't being followed. It had been Sophie's opinion that if Thorp Kingman didn't chase after her, then when he knew her car had gone he would naturally assume she had gone too.

And so he might, she thought, but since some brilliant radar had taken him to the house where his niece was, wasn't it just as likely that that same radar would track Sophie down to her flat? Lord knew how he had found her. She could spend the rest of the night puzzling that one out. Reaching her flat, and just in case, she shunted her own car out of the garage, then drove the Morgan in. Just supposing Thorp Kingman had found Sophie by cruising around London in his car and had spotted the Morgan parked outside Primrose's house, she was taking the precaution of tucking the car out of sight.

Wondering what time she might see her, though Sophie had told her not to wait up for her in case she had to devise another plan according to circumstances and could well stay overnight at some hotel, Jancis stepped out of the lift on her floor—and then all thoughts of Sophie and Thorp Kingman went from her mind. For there, asleep, sitting with his legs stretched out in front of him, his back propped up against her door, was Davy Venables, the fourth of their youthful quartet, a man the same twenty-four years as her brother, a dear, dear friend whom she hadn't seen for twelve months. Propped up beside him was the same easel and rucksack he must carry everywhere he went.

'Davy.' She woke him gently.

He opened his eyes, brown and twinkling the way she remembered them. 'Can I cadge a bed for the night?' he asked. Then he was on his feet, his long thin arms round her as he hugged her with the familiarity of long-standing friends.

'Not so much as a card do I get!' she admonished him, unlocking the door and welcoming him inside. 'Hungry?'

'Beans on toast?' he replied.

While Davy sat in the kitchen and, always hungry, tucked into his beans on toast, Jancis scooted round changing the sheets on her bed. Davy had better have her room, she decided. If Sophie did turn up tonight and let herself in with the spare key she had given her, then it would be better for them to bunk in together in William's room rather than to have her charging into that same room and letting out a shriek that would rouse the whole block of flats when she saw Davy's black curly mop sticking out from under the covers. Davy looked as though he needed all the sleep he could get, and Sophie could talk to him in the morning.

Over a hot drink he told her he had hitch-hiked from Cornwall that day and was off again in the morning, meeting some friends at Victoria Coach Station. From there they were off to Paris.

'Enjoying life, Davy?' she asked. Davy's father was not as affluent as hers and Sophie's. She doubted he had an allowance at all, but it had never bothered him.

'You bet,' he said. 'There's this girl . . .' He stopped, and she realised he must think a lot of 'this girl' but was sensitive about bringing his feelings out into the open. She knew how he felt, she had felt like that about Shaw, and hadn't even told William.

'Serious?' she asked gently.

'*I* am,' he said, leaving it there, and having already learned that he had missed seeing William by less than twenty-four hours, he asked, 'See anything of Sophie?'

'Funny you should ask that,' said Jancis, and told him of the interruption she had received in her well ordered life that day.

'Bloody nut case,' was Davy's fond opinion, for he loved Sophie; they all did. 'Though as I remember, you weren't above getting into hot water yourself in the old days.'

'You make us sound as if we should be drawing our pensions,' she said, and he grinned.

'If I remember correctly, wasn't it this same Thorp Kingman who whaled your backside that time . . .'

'The trouble with honorary brothers, Davy Venables,'

said Jancis with an attempt at loftiness, 'is that they never have any sensitivity to the hurt pride of one's youth.'

Not much later, with Davy from the look of him already asleep in the other bedroom, Jancis lay wakeful, recalling that day she had vowed to hate Thorp Kingman for as long as she lived.

It had been during the school holidays, she remembered; she did not recall what had gone on before, just remembered the four of them had been ambling up the Ellingtons' long drive.

'Wow!' Davy had exclaimed, as they neared the house. 'Get a look at that!'

All eyes had turned in the direction he was pointing. As far as she was concerned there was nothing to get excited about in the shiny black limousine parked outside the house. But the two boys seemed to think it was something special as they argued about the make.

The four of them had gone nearer to have a closer inspection. 'Whose is it?' William had asked.

'It belongs to Thorp,' Sophie stated, and none of them had thought to question who Thorp was.

'Boy, would I like to drive that,' Davy enthused, thirteen years old and beginning to take an interest in anything mechanical.

'You couldn't move it without the ignition keys,' William had pointed out knowledgeably.

'I could,' Sophie piped up, only to be shot down in flames by the boys.

'So could I,' she remembered chipping in, taking Sophie's side since the ungentlemanly squashing of the other two had made her friend look tearful. And knowing that since she had the attention of three pairs of eyes she was going to have to prove her boast, she added, 'It's easy.'

Without more ado she had the car door open and was inside searching for the handbrake. Her mother picked her up from school most days, she knew all about hand-brakes. The handbrake off, she felt the car roll forward on the slope of the drive. But she had miscalculated that slope, if she had thought about it at all, and instead of rolling to a stop the car had carried on. The 'What did I tell you' look she threw at the others changed to one of panic as the car started to gather momentum. Panic made her deaf to William's yell of, 'Put the handbrake on!' and she could only be thankful for his presence of mind that he ran with the car and yanked her out as it picked up speed.

In deathly silence they watched as, travelling in a straight line, ignoring the curve of the drive, the car went with deadly accuracy across the flower border and lawns, and headed for the boundary wall. The sickening sound of breaking glass told them it had come to a halt and that for sure at least one of the headlamps had had it.

No one moved as they stood, horrified. Then a strangled gasp left Sophie as a thunderous-looking giant, at least ten feet tall, Jancis remembered thinking at the time, came out of the house, his long legs quickly covering the ground as he went to inspect the damage. And then he turned, his look ferocious.

'Oh hell,' said the ten-year-old Sophie, having picked up the expression from somewhere. Then as the giant approached, 'Run for it!' she yelled, already on her way. Without hesitating William and Davy chased after her.

To give them the benefit of the doubt, they probably thought she was right behind them. Only she wasn't. As though turned to stone, she had stood terrified as the angry man had come up and looked down at her.

'Do you know anything about this?' he had asked very quietly, too quietly.

Jancis had been too frightened to lie. 'It was me,' she had gasped, trembling with fear. 'I let the handbrake off.'

He hadn't waited for any more but had picked up her

skinny form, placed her over his knee and administered, too many in her opinion, resounding slaps on her rear end.

Terror had fled. Fury and indignation sent it flying. How dared he! How *dared* he! Only last week her mother had had a private talk with her, had told her she was on her way to becoming a young lady, and here was this ogre treating her as though she was a kid. That she rarely remembered she was a young lady for more than ten minutes together had nothing to do with it.

Thorp Kingman set her to her feet and scanned her rebellious face. He looked as though he expected her to say something. But with her face scarlet, her green eyes shimmering with hate, she had stared back in silence. The memory came back to her that he had looked taken aback to see so much hate, as though had she shrieked her head off or started blubbering he could have understood it better. Then very slowly, absently almost, he had brushed a strand of titian hair back from her forehead and said quietly, perceptively:

'You beautiful child. I've hurt your dignity, haven't I?'

It wasn't until ages later that she had realised he could have been apologising for lathering her seat. But at that moment, refusing to cry though feeling more mentally bruised than physically for all she doubted she would be sitting down to lunch, she felt a rage she didn't know she had inside her spiral up and she didn't care that he thought her a beautiful child, because her mother had told her she was a young lady, and she had kicked out at him viciously with her sturdily shod foot. She had caught him a crack on the shin that made her wince to remember it, and had felt her vocal cords released.

'I hate you!' she had yelled. 'You mean—mean pig!'

She had raced off then, hoping with all her heart she had crippled him. That would teach him to up-end young ladies! He could have chased after her, she supposed, if she hadn't broken his shin. With those enormously long legs he could easily have caught up with her. But he hadn't followed, and the other three were waiting for her at the bottom of the drive. They had witnessed her shame in having her bottom paddled and she didn't feel like talking to them that they hadn't come to her rescue.

'Ooh, Jancy!' Sophie had wailed, near to tears in her sympathy.

'It didn't hurt,' she remembered saying haughtily, and had stalked off home with her head in the air. But it had hurt—had hurt for a long time. It had hurt so much she couldn't quite think when she had pushed it to the back of her mind.

Someone ringing at the front door bell brought her from sleep to a semi-conscious state. She vaguely heard voices, opened one eye to see it was daylight, opened the other to see that Sophie wasn't there, and decided Sophie had just arrived and was talking to Davy.

Still shedding sleep, the realisation that Sophie must have turned into an early riser if she had breakfasted in her hotel before coming on here penetrated. She'd better get up just in case Sophie hadn't eaten. And anyway, she'd like to be sure Davy had a decent breakfast inside him before he went.

She had just shrugged into her robe when, after the briefest of taps on the door, Davy opened it and popped his head round. 'Ah, you're up,' he said by way of good morning. 'You've got a visitor.'

'Put the kettle on, there's a love. I'm gasping for a cup of coffee,' she replied, going to the dressing table to drag a cursory brush through her tangled locks.

Her face free of make-up, a look of sleep still about her, her titian hair still managing to look tousled, Jancis went along the hall and into the sitting room. And there she stopped, her intention of going on into the kitchen never materialising. For her visitor wasn't the one she had been fully expecting to see.

Drawing her flimsy covering more firmly around her, she found herself face to face with none other than a man she knew to be cold, hard and not above spanking a twelve-year-old should the misdemeanour in his view call for such punishment. Somehow or other Thorp Kingman had traced her, and the look on his face was telling her that in his opinion, when he'd had her over his knee that time, he hadn't hit her half hard enough.

CHAPTER THREE

ALL too conscious that her appearance showed she had just got out of bed, though since it couldn't be very much past eight and she had been to a party the night before, Jancis didn't think she warranted a black mark. She became annoyed that already she was looking for excuses with which to defend herself against this glowering man, and advanced farther into the room. Angry to find herself on the defensive, she threw Thorp Kingman a cool look that belied her feelings.

'Would you care to take a seat, Mr Kingman?' she said in her best hostess manner. 'I'll be with you directly. I have a guest . . .' She left the words trailing in the air as she turned towards the kitchen intending to go in search of Davy. Before she had moved a couple of yards, however, Davy emerged from the kitchen.

'Have to dash,' he said, 'I'm going to be late otherwise.'

'Oh,' she said, disappointed. Davy had looked so tired last night that she hadn't kept him out of bed too long in catching up on his news. Without any regard for fairness, she blamed Thorp Kingman that because of him she wouldn't now have a chance to catch up with what Davy had been doing over the last twelve months. William too would have been interested to know how Davy was faring when she wrote to him. 'What about breakfast?' she asked, her plan to send him on his way with a plate of bacon and eggs under his belt fading.

'Fixed myself something, love,' he said.

She half turned with him and saw Thorp Kingman was still standing, having ignored her invitation to sit down.

His look told her he was becoming impatient too; hostility emanated from every pore. Whether or not Davy picked up the hostility too she didn't know, but she saw a wicked gleam enter his eyes and knew from the years of knowing him that he was about to make some remark that was guaranteed to have her wanting to box his ears.

'I'll be off then,' he said with an innocent smile in the direction of Sophie's uncle. Then, turning to Jancis, 'Thanks for the use of your bed—it's the best night I've had in ages.'

There was only one interpretation Thorp Kingman was going to put on that, Jancis thought, inwardly blessing Davy. She flicked a glance at her unwanted visitor and saw from the contemptuous glance he threw at her that he had gathered she and Davy had spent the night in each other's arms.

Smiling sweetly, she turned her glance back to Davy and witnessed the bland expression he was affecting, though nothing could take away that twinkling look in his eyes. 'I hope your rabbits die!' she muttered so only he could hear. Then more loudly, 'I'll see you out.'

'Thanks for nothing,' she told him when she had him in the hall, the door to the sitting room closed.

'You're not mad, are you?' he questioned hurriedly. 'It was so obvious what old sobersides in there was thinking, so I thought I'd show him neither of us cared about his opinion. But if his opinion *does* bother you I'll go and put him straight.'

'Don't be daft,' she said, then realising it could be another twelve months before she saw Davy again and wanting to have no cause for dissent between them, 'I don't care a fig for his opinion.'

'Sure?'

'Positive.'

Davy paused, trying to read the truth from her eyes. 'Well, so long, love,' he said, and with a schoolboy grin peeping out, 'I'll try to remember to send you a postcard from Paris!'

Returning to the sitting room, Jancis wished she had had the nerve to keep Thorp Kingman waiting a while longer while she got dressed. But from that taut look of impatience he wore, she had an idea that if she didn't join him soon after the front door closed, he could well come looking for her. She felt enough at a disadvantage without him finding her less dressed than she was.

He hadn't moved and wasted no time when she joined him in telling her without preamble, 'I'd like to see my niece.'

'I'm afraid you can't.' Futile to prevaricate and say she hadn't a clue who he was talking about. Already she had been too unaware in the cloak-and-dagger stuff Sophie practised and had called him Mr Kingman, so he knew she knew who he was. He favoured her with a look that told her 'Can't' was not in his dictionary. He confirmed it.

'Can't, Miss Langfield?'

'H-how do you know she's here?' she replied, intending to back Sophie to the hilt in her intention not to go to the home of this sour-looking individual, though knowing herself hopeless in the art of duplicity.

'Are you saying she isn't? You have two bedrooms, don't you?'

He didn't miss a thing, did he? He must have counted the doors leading off the hall when Davy had let him in and duly ticked off in his mind what each room housed. Oddly Jancis found herself thinking what a nice mouth he had. Though his top lip was tight with restraint, his lower lip had a sensuality to it. She couldn't help thinking his mouth would take on a certain warmth if ever he so far as forgot himself and allowed those lips to curve into a smile.

'*Is* she here?' he demanded, his eyes following the

direction of hers, his bottom lip taking on a taut line too.

Grief, he'll be thinking I'm setting my cap at *him* next! she thought, bringing her focus rapidly away from a mouth that was showing tightly controlled anger.

'Yes, she's here,' she lied, badly wanting to shiver from the icy blast in those cold grey eyes. 'But she isn't very well,' she added hastily when Thorp made an irritated movement and looked as if he had finished with the niceties of asking her permission and seemed ready to search the flat himself until he found his errant niece. 'We went to a party last night,' she tacked on needlessly, and wished she hadn't when he rounded on her.

'I was there,' he snapped, adding, nastily she thought, 'And if you think I'm going to leave Sophie here with the likes of you, then you're very much mistaken!'

Her face flushed scarlet at that. Oh, how she wished she hadn't reminded him. She couldn't blame him, of course, though she could have done without her sense of fairness taking just that moment to wake up. But had she been in charge of a lively twenty-one-year-old, would she sanction her staying with an older girl she had seen for herself on a bed looking to be in the throes of being made love to? Had heard with her own ears less than twelve hours later another man intimating that they had spent a very enjoyable night together? One look at Thorp Kingman's face told her that any explanation she made would be scorned. He was probably already blaming her for the invented hangover she had excused Sophie with.

His patience came to a sudden and abrupt end. He was past bandying words with her. 'Tell my niece to be here ready, at midday, for me to take her to my home,' he instructed her icily. 'Also tell her that if she has any plans to give me the run around, any idea of not being here when I call to collect her, then not only will I wash my hands of her, but I shall immediately cable her parents.'

Poor, poor Sophie, Jancis thought a second later, as the

sound of the hall door slamming reverberated in her ears. He had been as mad as hell! She had never thought herself poor-spirited, but as Thorp had thundered his instructions to an end, the 'Yes, sir' she had wanted to answer had been lost under the glare of his eyes. The man was a monster! And poor Sophie had to put up with scenes like that for a whole month!

She went into the kitchen to make herself a steadying cup of coffee, her hands shaking as she reached to reheat the kettle Davy had boiled for her. Her coffee just made, her hands still shaking, she heard the sound of a latch key in the front door, and was in the hall before Sophie had the door closed behind her.

'You've had a gentleman caller.' Sophie got in before her. 'Crikey, that was a close shave! The lift doors had almost shut when I saw Thorp storm by. He didn't see me, thank goodness.' Unspeaking, Jancis led the way into the sitting room. 'Golly, you look pale,' Sophie observed. 'Did he wipe the floor with you?'

'He's coming back at twelve o'clock—It'll be your turn then.'

'He'll be lucky,' said Sophie, her good spirits rising to the surface as she congratulated herself on having missed him. 'I'll be away by . . .'

'He said he would cable your parents if you weren't here,' Jancis said, feeling suddenly very flat.

'*What!*' Sophie squeaked. 'Oh, crumbs! They'll stop my allowance for over a year if he does that.'

Over coffee Jancis related every word Sophie's uncle had said to her. She left nothing out, apart from the tussle she'd had with Vance Kettering that Thorp Kingman had misconstrued, letting her think that Davy's idiotic remark was the reason for him thinking she wasn't a fit person for her to stay with.

Sophie was put out at having missed seeing Davy, but she was highly indignant of the slur Thorp had put on her friend's character. 'I'm more likely to have a go at corrupting you than the other way around,' she said stoutly with charming honesty. 'I'll put him right about you, Jancy,' she promised sincerely. 'The very next time I see him I'll . . .'

'You'll be here when he comes back?'

'I shall have to be, shan't I? Apart from shortening the parents' holiday if he cables them, and he never says anything he doesn't mean, then they're bound to fly back ready to put the thumb-screws on the minute they get his wire. Mother had that look in her eye when they were talking about cutting off my allowance which means she won't let Dad be softened up when I turn on the water-works.'

Sophie was incorrigible, Jancis thought as the hands of the clock moved steadily on. She had lent a hand with the general chores, seeming determined to put a bright face on it, for all Jancis had caught her looking very pensive several times. They had both bathed and changed into jeans and sweaters and she had helped Sophie to repack everything she had unpacked yesterday.

It was during the course of one of their various conversations that Sophie enlightened her as to how Thorp Kingman had tracked them down to the party. It only solved half the mystery, but Sophie told her she would let her know the other half as soon as she had found out herself.

'Apparently, though don't ask me why, Thorp came to your flat looking for me.'

'Here?' Jancis exclaimed, and half to herself, 'Why here?' She had recalled vividly her one and only meeting with him eleven years ago, but he wouldn't have remembered, would he? He wouldn't have remembered and assumed she and Sophie had kept that friendship up, would he? 'He wouldn't know you and I are friends, would he?' she asked the question out loud. 'I mean, I rarely see you these days.'

'I could have mentioned your name on one of the visits to his house the parents drag me to from time to time, I suppose,' Sophie said thoughtfully.

'Yes,' Jancis conceded, 'but you wouldn't have told him my address, would you?'

'Most unlikely,' Sophie replied. 'And clever as he is, he'd need the help of a crystal ball to know I'd invited myself to stay with you.' She was thoughtful again, then dismissing the puzzle of how Thorp had found the address, she said, 'To get back to what I was saying. When I saw from Primrose's bedroom window that Thorp's car had gone, I thought it was safe to come out of hiding.' At this point a reflective grin popped out. 'So I went back and joined the party.'

'You didn't!' said Jancis, and when the other nodded wickedly, 'Honestly, Sophie, you take the biscuit!'

'I know,' said Sophie happily. 'Anyway, I had a super time. A good few of us stayed to breakfast,' she went on, and would have said more, having revealed that she hadn't gone to a hotel for the night as Jancis had thought, but she seemed to realise Jancis was impatient to know more of how her uncle had traced them.

'As I said, Thorp called here, and so,' she added, 'did a certain gent named Adrian.'

'Adrian? Adrian Hayward?'

'Hmm,' said Sophie. 'Apparently you make Adrian's heart go pitter-pat. Anyway, he'd been to the party, seen you hadn't arrived, and took it into his head to call for you in case your car had broken down or some such.'

It was clear then what had happened after that. 'He met your uncle here . . .'

'Outside your very door.'

'One word led to another . . .'

'And hey presto, poor Primrose has got two uninvited guests.'

Jancis had to laugh, though it wasn't really funny. Not when she considered the opinion Thorp Kingman had of her. Then gradually as the minutes ticked by, the more she thought of Thorp Kingman, the more a slow burning anger against him began to make itself felt. And suddenly, where before fair-mindedness had neutralised her sometimes volatile temper, she was livid. She took care not to let Sophie see how she was feeling, but as the time neared noon she called herself all sorts of a worm for not letting fly at him when she had had him in earshot. It niggled away at her that she had kept quiet when Thorp had called her 'the likes of you'. How she'd like to see him eat dirt, like to see him get his come-uppance!

The old remembered hurt of eleven years ago stoked the fire. She had hated him then. That went double now. Oh, if only there was some way she could get back at him! There wasn't any way, of course, but if there was, wouldn't she just jump at the chance!

Sophie again bringing up the subject of Davy had her leaving her private thoughts of what she would like to do to one Thorp Kingman. But when Sophie asked her to let her explain to him about Davy, some sense, perhaps of inverted pride that said if he wanted to think that about her, then let him, had her saying, 'No.'

'Are you sure?' asked Sophie. 'I mean, he'll feel all sorts of a heel for jumping to the wrong conclusions, won't he? Oh, let me tell him, Jancy. It'll be lovely to see his face.'

'I'd rather he didn't know,' Jancis said firmly. Even if Sophie did tell him, there was still her tussle with Vance Kettering unaccounted for, and one man less wouldn't make Thorp Kingman think any differently about her.

'All right,' Sophie agreed, then, her impish grin coming to the fore, 'You must be enjoying a "scarlet woman" phase.'

The clock had barely shown twelve when there was a ring at the door.

'Prepare to meet your doom,' Sophie intoned, though she didn't look nearly as cheerful as she was trying to sound.

'I'll wait in William's bedroom,' said Jancis, not wanting to see Thorp Kingman ever again. 'You can come and say cheerio when you come in for your cases.'

'Oh, Jancy, don't leave me alone with him. I've got to put up with him for a month,' Sophie wailed, looking tearful. 'At least stay with me until I have to go.'

Sophie always had had the knack of turning tears on at will. But even so, the thought of the month the poor girl had in front of her softened her resolution, not trusting her own reaction, to put herself out of reach of Thorp Kingman's sharp tongue. She hesitated, and the door bell pealed impatiently again.

'Please!' Sophie pleaded, a tear falling to her cheek.

'Oh, all right,' she said, not at all as graciously as she could have done.

Sophie wiped her damp cheek, and magically her tears dried. Jancis turned from her and went out into the hall. It needed a deep calming breath before she opened the door.

Dressed as he had been before, in slacks and sweater, Thorp Kingman stood there. Without saying a word he stepped into the hall, and with her lips tight shut, Jancis left him to follow her.

'Hello, Thorp,' Sophie said huskily as he walked into the sitting room. Then, with a charm few could resist, though her uncle seemed to be immune, she said, 'I've been a naughty girl, haven't I?'

Incorrigible wasn't the word, Jancis thought, though she couldn't help admiring Sophie's act in the face of the stern displeasure that was coming her way.

'Are you ready?' he asked, in a voice that said woe betide her if she wasn't. He looked about him. 'Do you have a suitcase anywhere?'

'I have a headache,' said Sophie, and looking at her, though this was the first time a headache had been mentioned, Jancis saw that she was indeed looking a little washed out. Her sympathy already on its way, she drew it back, biting her lip in an effort not to smile. No wonder Sophie looked washed out; she had been enjoying herself so much at the party, she hadn't been to bed yet.

'So do I have a headache,' said an unsympathetic uncle. 'It goes by the name of Sophie Ellington. A couple of aspirins will sort yours out, mine won't be cured until these next four weeks are over.'

With amazement, Jancis saw that Sophie was amused by her uncle's satirical humour. 'I really do have a headache,' she groaned, turning her face away from him. 'There's a 'flu bug going round. Do you think I could have 'flu?'

Having been totally ignored up to now, Jancis moved forward. She saw what Sophie's game was. If she could convince him that she might be sickening for 'flu, not wanting to be bothered with having an invalid on his hands, he might consider leaving her to her caring hands. Thorp Kingman observed that she had moved nearer to his niece, but had no words to waste on her.

'No, I do not think you have 'flu,' he said stonily. 'The only thing wrong with you, young lady, is a giant-sized hangover, and from what I saw being tipped into the punch bowl at that party last night, it surprises me that both of you aren't clutching ice bags to your heads. But then some people are more used than others to knocking back drink night after night and they become immune to the effects.'

That he was perfectly aware that she was still in the room, that his jibe had been intended for her, had anger exploding within Jancis. 'I'm the one who's surprised, Mr Kingman,' she stated with remarkable cool considering she was so angry. 'In fact I would go as far as to say not surprised, but shocked. How I got the impression I can't think, but somehow I gained the idea that you were far too virtuous to have ever had a hangover, much less to know that an ice bag can give some relief.'

Thorp Kingman killed her with a look, then ignored her as he turned his attention back to Sophie. 'I've wasted enough time,' he told her. 'Where's your case?'

'In the bedroom. I'll get it,' she said, standing up. 'Ooh!' she gasped, swaying towards him. 'Oh, Thorp, I do feel peculiar!'

The seething fury Jancis had been experiencing disappeared, and alarm gripped her when she saw how pale Sophie had gone. Thorp Kingman witnessed her pallor too, and the two of them were suddenly united in helping Sophie to sit down again.

'It doesn't look like a hangover to me,' said Jancis, more to herself than anything.

'I haven't felt well for the last couple of days,' Sophie said in a little voice. 'My throat feels sore.'

Unsure whether she was faking—she'd been fine up until about ten minutes ago, Jancis recalled—though one couldn't change the colour of one's complexion just like that, could one?—she went hurrying for the aspirin and a glass of water. When she returned, it was Thorp Kingman who took the glass and tablets from her and administered them to his niece.

'I'll be fine once I'm tucked up in bed,' Sophie said bravely.

'I'll drive as quickly as circumstances permit,' she was told.

Sophie winced, but whether it was because her head was throbbing, or whether it was because she was realising that, ill or not, he was still insisting on taking her with him when he left, Jancis couldn't be sure. Then Sophie said something that absolutely took her breath away, and she too felt like wincing that her friend could be so cruel as to suggest such a thing.

'Can Jancy come with us to look after me?' she asked, her voice frail. 'She has such lovely cool hands.'

Instantly Jancis took her hands away from Sophie's forehead. Though after that first shock from her words she realised she had nothing to worry about. Thorp Kingman didn't want her in his home any more than she wanted to go there. He would never entertain the thought of allowing the sort of girl he thought she was to cross his threshold. It would, though, be interesting to see how he got out of it. She left him to reply to Sophie.

'You can't expect your friend to drop everything at a moment's notice,' he told her, not once looking in Jancis's direction.

'You wouldn't mind, would you, Jancy?' Sophie raised tear-filled eyes to appeal to her.

'Miss Langfield most likely has a full engagement book,' he said, not giving Jancis the time to reply.

He looked at her then and a rush of supreme delight flooded through her that he was positively squirming as he tried, tactfully in front of his niece, to get out of having her as a guest in his home.

She couldn't hope to hide that her green eyes were dancing with delight, though the rest of her was extremely cool as she stretched out a deliberate pause, knowing they were both waiting for her answer—the one to hear she would go, the other certain she would claim she would be far too socially busy to go with them.

Her timing perfect, she looked from Thorp to the pleading look of Sophie, and then, trying not to laugh as she visualised the effect her words would have on him, she said:

'I haven't a thing planned. And if poor Sophie *is* in for 'flu, then I really do think I should be the one to nurse her. After all, what are friends for?'

She left it there, sternly repressed laughter bubbling

inside as she waited for Thorp to 'get out of that'. Of course she hadn't any intention of going within a mile of his home. But oh, the pleasure in watching him wriggle! She watched the ice form in his eyes, saw those glacial eyes narrow as he studied her wide-eyed, sweetly innocent face. But she was enjoying too much the feeling of having notched up a score, if only a tiny one, against him to dampen down her elation.

'In that case,' he said, and she was still too happily crowing to be wary, 'I would be delighted to have you as my house guest.'

'What!' The horrified exclamation came before she could stop it, her cool demeanour shattered. 'But . . .' He wasn't serious? He couldn't be? Yet somehow she knew that he was. Knew also that he had sensed she had declared war on him; he had a light of battle in his eyes anyway. And also, as he surveyed her flabbergasted expression, she knew he had entered the first skirmish and come out the victor.

'Something wrong?' he enquired, his look changing to one of mockery. 'Have you suddenly remembered a pressing engagement?'

Oh how she wished it was in her nature to walk away from a fight. 'Not at all,' she said, managing to keep her voice even when she was inwardly boiling with frustrated rage. Her self-congratulations on having begun to work off the score she had to settle with him had, she saw, been totally much too previous. 'I was just wondering about cancelling the milk—that sort of thing.'

He didn't bat an eyelid that his unwilling invitation had been accepted, though he did turn his head to look at Sophie—probably, Jancis guessed, to check if she really *was* as ill as she claimed to be.

She looked at her too and saw that Sophie had rested her head on the wing of the chair, a look of sleepy innocence about her, that was just too innocent to be true.

CHAPTER FOUR

JANCIS was still seething when Thorp Kingman steered his car out of London half an hour later. Matters were not helped at all by the fact that a sleepy-eyed Sophie, already looking better, had declared that if she could have the back seat to herself she could stretch out and rest better that way. That meant she had to sit in front beside the man who, apart from asking permission in her flat to ring his housekeeper to get a room ready for her, had said not another word to her.

He drove speedily and well. And she hated that about him too. Hated that everything he did seemed to have an air of confidence about it. Sophie too came in for some of her anger, tucked up as she was in the back sleeping like a baby with nothing on her conscience. She was covered with a blanket Thorp had supplied and resting her head comfortably on cushions from the flat. They had both had a hand in mollycoddling her, and Jancis was growing more and more angrily certain there was nothing wrong with her that eight hours' sleep wouldn't cure.

They were almost within sight of the village of Abbotts Hanley where Thorp had his home before she had cooled down sufficiently to allow her sense of fair play to soften her anger. Sophie was just Sophie. She was no different from the bundle of T.N.T. she had always been. Sophie being Sophie was why every one was so fond of her. And really Jancis couldn't blame her for not wanting to be shut away alone with her un-fun-loving uncle until her parents returned.

As for Thorp Kingman, the morose man by her side who appeared to have taken a vow of silence—well, what had she expected? She had challenged him, had been cockily sure he would duck that challenge and had found to her cost that he had put aside his personal feelings about her and had taken her up on her challenge.

She didn't like him any better now than she had when they had started out. But having taken one or two surreptitious glances at him as they drove along, she saw from that firm aggressive chin that you only tangled with men like Thorp Kingman if you were sure you held all four aces. Not that that would stop her from trying to get the better of him if the opportunity arose; the scores she had to settle with him were mounting up.

As he turned the car into a drive that told her they had reached their destination, she flicked a glance at him. His hair was thick, dark and close cut as though he was determined to defy its tendency to wave, and oddly she found herself revising her earlier opinion of last night that he was not good-looking. There was definitely something about him that ... Hastily she turned her mind away from such treasonable thoughts. He was the enemy—he had nothing nice about him at all.

The car stopped in front of a large sprawling house where a lively lady somewhere in her forties, Jancis thought, tripped lightly down the stone steps. She was already out of the car, glad to be free from that grim silence, when the housekeeper reached them and was duly introduced as Mrs Hemmings.

Mrs Hemmings' round face smiled at her as Jancis extended her hand, then fairly beamed at the sleeping Sophie, who was being roused by her uncle.

'It will be lovely having two young ladies in the house!' she exclaimed, going forward in case Sophie needed her help.

'Sophie would brighten up anywhere,' Jancis replied tongue in cheek, and didn't miss the sharp look Thorp threw her way as it reached him that she was implying that life at Widefields Manor must be deadly dull.

It pleased her to think she had niggled him, but he had a fine line of his own in ignoring her. He lost no time in getting them all indoors, telling her to leave the two heavy cases she had deliberately packed in order for him to see she wasn't going to be any mayfly visitor.

He left them at the bottom of the stairs, and Mrs Hemmings took them up to their rooms. Probably gone to drown his sorrows, Jancis thought gleefully, and only just stopped herself from whistling a merry tune as she followed in the wake of Mrs Hemmings, who had a ministering arm around Sophie's waist as she helped her to her room.

'I'll help Sophie into bed if you like,' Jancis offered, when she saw that was the housekeeper's first priority, and thinking that with an extra guest she hadn't anticipated Mrs Hemmings probably had other chores she wanted to attend to.

'That's all right, Miss Langfield,' Mrs Hemmings told her with a smile. 'I was an S.R.N. before circumstances forced me to give up nursing, and I enjoy putting my training to use.'

Mrs Hemmings hadn't told her what the circumstances were which had forced her to give up nursing, but just then Jancis was too stunned to show an interest. What on earth was she doing here if Mrs Hemmings was a State Registered Nurse? She knew less than nothing about nursing 'flu, if that really was what was wrong with Sophie, and she had an idea Thorp Kingman knew she was a stranger to nursing beyond holding foreheads and unscrewing caps from aspirin bottles. Yet here in his own home he had a qualified nurse! He must know of his housekeeper's qualifications too, since the valuable paintings she had seen on the way upstairs would certainly mean he had taken up references for anyone in his employ.

'Sorry to keep you waiting,' Mrs Hemmings apologised, firmly tucking a sleepy Sophie up in bed. 'Miss Ellington was looking in need of her bed, so I thought it best to get her settled first. If you'd like to come with me, I'll show you to your room. I've laid a light lunch in the dining room.'

Nothing, Jancis thought, would get her going down to the dining room while Sophie was up here in bed. She'd starve rather than sit at a table in the solitary company of Thorp Kingman. Mrs Hemmings was already on her way to the door as she told her she wasn't hungry. Following after her, Jancis turned to give one last look at her friend, intending to say she would see her later, but the words died on her lips as she saw Sophie, with a careful eye on Mrs Hemmings' departing back, suddenly switch her look back to her and then, moving her mouth expressively to one side, wink.

Honestly, Sophie was the limit! she thought, sternly keeping her mouth firm when her lips went to take an upward tilt as she went with Mrs Hemmings. At times Sophie made her furious, and it was annoying that she couldn't help wanting to laugh. As she had suspected, there was nothing wrong with her but exhaustion, and that wasn't entirely surprising since the bed she was now reposing in, having taken all Mrs Hemmings' cosseting with every semblance of being an invalid, was the first time she had been to bed since she had left her parents' home yesterday.

The room Mrs Hemmings had shown Jancis into was much the same as the one Sophie had. It was a large room, light and airy, having built-in wardrobes either side of a vanity table. Her suitcases had been brought up while she had been in Sophie's room, and wondering which of the many clothes she had brought with her to unpack, she decided to go the whole hog and unpack the lot. That way, should Thorp come in and look in the wardrobes, though for the life of her she couldn't think why he should, he would see it looked as though she had every intention of being here for a very long stay.

That thought caused her to wonder how brief she could make her stay without it looking as though she was leaving at the first opportunity. She would have to stay tonight anyway. But if Sophie had any idea about having a long and protracted illness, then Sophie was going to have to think again!

But when she went along to see Sophie several hours later, time having begun to hang heavily on her hands with her unpacking finished, the book she had brought with her unable to sustain her interest, and it being unthinkable that she go downstairs and risk putting herself in the company of Thorp Kingman, she discovered that Sophie had already tired of being ill. The few hours' sleep she had had were all Sophie required to bring her back to top form and she was now wide awake and ready for anything.

'Thank goodness you've come!' she exclaimed. 'I daren't get out of bed to come and look for you in case Thorp was anywhere around. I was just wondering if I threw a boot at the wall if that would bring you.'

'I'm not next door,' Jancis told her.

'Oh well, you're here now. Are you mad with me?'

'I should be,' said Jancis with an attempt at severity.

'But you're not. Good-oh. I did feel dizzy for a moment back at your flat, though,' Sophie said in an attempt to coax her friend out of her solemn expression. Then with that honesty that never failed to charm, 'But that was only because I'd been out on the tiles all night. I must have danced twenty miles!'

Jancis tried to take her to task for the way she had inveigled her in her plans, but found she couldn't be serious with her for very long, simply because Sophie refused to take anything very seriously and made all her objections to her suggestion that she accompany her to Widefields Manor sound very mean had she indeed been ill.

'I thought, when you told me not to tell him the truth about Davy that there was some needle going on between you and Thorp,' Sophie said idly. 'I thought that with your spirit you'd take any opportunity to have a go at him.' Her eyes gleamed with delight. 'You shouldn't have tried to back him into a corner the way you did, though, Jancy, by that challenging way you told him you had nothing on to prevent you coming with us.'

'I shouldn't?'

'Nuh-uh,' Sophie grunted. 'Though perhaps I should have warned you that just when you think you have Thorp scuttled, he has the uncanniest knack of reversing the situation, and wham, it's you that's over a barrel. And while you're still wondering what went wrong, you find that you're the one who's dancing to heel and that that uncle of mine is the one who's pulling the strings.'

Jancis mused over what Sophie had said, not liking the thought of being anyone's puppet. Sophie had admitted she knew there was some needle going on between her and Thorp, yet had asked if she could come and nurse her knowing he wouldn't care for the idea. Sophie knew her well, had known she would challenge him when he tried to get out of the invitation. And from what she had just told her, she knew full well that Thorp was equal to flooring her.

'You deliberately set me up, didn't you?' she accused stiffly. And when Sophie tried to look contrite but failed, 'You wretch!' she added with feeling.

'Don't be cross with me, Jancy,' Sophie pleaded, working hard to hold back a grin, 'I'm only little.' Jancis knew she was fighting a losing battle to stay angry with her. 'Stay up here and have dinner,' Sophie urged. 'You can help me invent some reason for a sudden recovery. I'm not staying in bed tomorrow, that's for sure.'

Before she could reply that in her view Sophie would be less likely to get herself or any other unsuspecting soul into mischief if she stayed in bed till her parents came home, the door opened and Thorp came in. He had changed into a superbly cut dark grey suit, and made a semblance of greeting Jancis politely before turning his attention to his niece.

'How are you now?' he enquired, his eyes scrutinising her face, but his expression inscrutable.

'Oh, much better, Thorp,' Sophie said quietly. 'My headache's gone, and it doesn't hurt to swallow any more.'

'Must be something in the air here to effect so spontaneous a cure,' he murmured, causing Jancis to suspect he had never for an instant believed his niece's lies about having 'flu.

Though that didn't make sense! If he had known all along there was nothing wrong with her, then why for heaven's sake had he agreed that she should come to look after her? It made as much sense as the fact that she was here, knowing next to nothing about nursing, when he already had a trained nurse on the premises.

'We'll see how you feel after having a few days in bed,' he went on urbanely, not missing, she was sure, the way Sophie's eyes flew wide at the very suggestion.

But all she said was a meek, 'Yes, Thorp.' Then he was turning his attention to his other unwanted guest.

'Your room is comfortable?' he enquired in the manner of the perfect host, his eyes taking in the beautiful texture of her skin, flicking for the briefest of moments to her eminently kissable mouth.

'Yes, thank you,' she replied, in the manner of the perfect guest.

'Good,' he said briefly, already on his way to the door. 'I shall be going out later this evening, but will be dining at home. Perhaps you'll join me in the drawing room for a drink before we eat.'

She couldn't help admiring the smooth sophistication of his invitation to dine with him, for all she didn't want to admire anything about him.

'Would you mind very much if I didn't?' she asked, and not waiting for his round of applause, went on, 'If it's no trouble to Mrs Hemmings I thought I would have dinner up here with Sophie.'

Sophie burst out laughing when Thorp had gone, not having missed that sparks were barely beneath the surface of the civility with which he and Jancis spoke to each other.

'I've always admired your spirit, Jancy,' she said, 'but I reckon you've taken on a tough one there.'

'We were perfectly polite,' Jancis replied, wanting to dampen down Sophie's idea that she and her uncle were at daggers drawn. Sophie just couldn't be trusted to leave them to get on with their private war.

Not wanting to make too much extra work for Mrs Hemmings, she offered to go down to collect their meal trays, only to be told by Sophie that besides Mrs Hemmings having the help of Carol, a girl who came from the village most mornings, Thorp invariably arranged for a Mrs Craven to come in early evenings when he had company staying.

This proved to be the case, and it was after Mrs Craven had been in to collect their used dishes, when Sophie was extracting information from Jancis about some of the people she had met at the party last night, that Sophie suddenly said:

'Oh help! I forgot. I've got a date tonight.'

As far as Jancis could see, she didn't look too put out about it, though since she had forgotten she had a date, the man in question couldn't be all that important to her.

Sophie consulted her watch. 'Quarter to nine,' she

announced. 'I expect he's already left to pick me up at your flat.'

'My flat!'

'Mmmm. I met him at the party. I suppose I could try ringing him up,' she said, her eyes going to the bedroom extension. 'If I knew his number . . .' She laughed lightly. 'If I knew his other name it would be a help too. Perhaps you know him, Jancy. Tommy something or other. Ginger hair . . .'

'Tommy Miller,' Jancis supplied, and when Sophie looked expectantly at her, 'Sorry, I haven't a clue about his telephone number.'

'Thorp must have a London telephone directory. Go down and get it, there's a love,' Sophie urged. 'You might recognise his address and it's only good manners to at least try and contact him. Thorp hates bad manners,' she tacked on for no reason Jancis could see.

But it wasn't that that startled her, or the fact of being a guest of someone who seemed to set a high value on good manners. What did startle her was that there had been a definite note of affection in Sophie's voice when she had spoken of Thorp.

'I thought you didn't like him—Thorp, I mean,' she said taken aback.

'I never said that!' Sophie gasped. 'He's great most of the time. It's just this house with it's stuffy antiques I can't stand. That, plus the fact that it's miles from any sign of life,' she exaggerated, 'added to the fact that Thorp doesn't take his responsibilities lightly and that if I want to freak out while I'm here, then I know before I start that I'm going to end up being in dead trouble.' She broke off to urge, 'Go and get that directory, Jan, we're wasting time.'

Jancis was thoughtful as she went down the stairs, wondering how she had got it so completely wrong. She tried to remember anything Sophie had said to give her the impression she had received that, like her, Sophie thought he was hateful. She'd definitely said she would have to put up with him for a month; implying by that that there was no love lost. But she saw then that what Sophie had really meant was that she would have to put up with Thorp breathing down her neck every time she took a step out of line.

Having thought Thorp would have gone out by now, Jancis had a foot on the bottom stair when one of the doors off the wide hall opened and a very good-looking blonde woman of about thirty preceded him from the room. Oh hell, she thought, it was too late to dash back upstairs and come back in a few minutes, they had seen her. She took the last stair and stood in the hall as Thorp and his companion came up to her.

For one of the few times in her life she experienced a feeling of inadequacy as she caught the sophisticated blonde giving her the once-over. She felt like a street urchin in her jeans and sweater opposite the fur coat that topped the long dress of the other woman. It was obvious they were on their way out, equally obvious that Thorp had never intended to dine *à deux* with her. The blonde had been his partner at dinner, so she would have been an unwanted third.

Thorp introduced the blonde as Aileen Forbes, and, about to extend her hand, Jancis saw she had no intention of shaking hands with her. Thinking them a pair well matched, she went to slide past them. If she was right the kitchen lay to the right, and she didn't want to stay in the hall searching for the telephone directories with them still there.

'Can I help you with anything?' Thorp asked, and Jancis wished he hadn't, because she wanted nothing from him, either help or his best host's good manners.

'I'm—er—looking for Mrs Hemmings,' she muttered.

'Mrs Hemmings will be attending to her invalid husband at the moment,' he told her, then as a sound of impatience came from Aileen Forbes, he turned to her and told her evenly, 'I won't be a moment, Aileen, perhaps you'd like to wait in the car.' He waited until she had gone through the door, then asked, 'Now, what's the problem?'

'I haven't got a problem,' Jancis stated coolly, refraining from adding, Not unless you can count trying to be civil to you. 'I want to make a telephone call, only I've forgotten the number.'

'So you're looking for the telephone directories,' he said, then walked from her to open a cupboard beneath the telephone table. 'Which one do you want?' he asked, bending down.

'London please, for M,' she said, trying to keep cool at the speculating look he gave her.

'Missing your men friends already, Jancis?' he enquired mockingly straightening up, the directory in his hands. Then his tone changed, hardened. 'Just don't try to corrupt my niece while you're here,' he said threateningly, and would, she thought, have said more, only her temper soared and she wasn't in a mind to stay and listen.

Her green eyes flashing, she snatched the directory from him and stormed back up the stairs. If she'd stayed another second she'd have hit him, she knew she would. She didn't like that remark any more than she liked him using her first name. He hadn't bothered to hide the fact that he thought had she been in London she would be spending this evening in a way very similar to the way he thought she had spent last night. It had taken a lot not to stand there and fire back at him. But one day, she thought, one day she was going to get even with him!

'Oh, good, you've got it,' said Sophie as soon as she went into her room.

Jancis waited only long enough to help Sophie find the correct telephone number, then asked if she would mind if she went to bed.

'I'm feeling tired again myself now,' Sophie declared, luxuriating in a yawn. 'Sometimes your ideas aren't too bad, Jancy.'

Jancis stirred, opened her eyes, noted the cup of tea that had been brought in, probably by the Carol Sophie had spoken of, then with the idea of going down for another five minutes, she closed her eyes. But she didn't get the chance of another five minutes, for the door burst open and Sophie was in the room.

'Mystery solved,' she announced, looking pretty in her floral quilted dressing gown and coming to perch herself on the edge of the bed.

'Mystery?' Jancis echoed, not yet up to coping with the ebullient Sophie, though trying for all that as she tucked a strand of titian hair behind her ear and waited expectantly.

'Thorp,' said Sophie briefly, which didn't explain anything, Jancis thought. 'You know—how he found out your address.'

Jancis was suddenly wide awake. 'You've discovered . . .'

'When I didn't show up here, Thorp rang home and spoke to Mrs Maynard, our housekeeper. She told him I'd been gone—with suitcases—for hours. He must have put her through the third degree, because she told him, would you believe, that she'd overheard me on the phone arranging to go and stay with someone called Jancy. I'll bet he was livid,' Sophie added, grinning.

'But how did he know where I lived? Mrs Maynard doesn't have my address, does she?'

'No, but you remember that birthday present I haven't given you yet? Well, I was in such a hurry to get out of there, I forgot it again.'

'You left it on the hall table,' Jancis remembered.

'And Mrs Maynard must have been speaking from the phone on the hall table. She'd have to be blind to have missed it. I wrote your full name and address in my best bold print.'

'So Mrs Maynard read Thorp my address . . .'

'And he went to your flat, met Adrian, and the rest we know.'

As Sophie had said, the mystery was solved, and she went on to tell Jancis Thorp had come to her room not long ago to find out how she was feeling this morning. 'Though more, I suspect, to see if I was still in residence,' Sophie opined, her face solemn for a moment. 'Though with the threat of him cabling my parents hanging over my head, I'm hardly likely to abscond. Still,' she said, her face brightening, 'we have the rest of the day to please ourselves what we do. Thorp will be glued to his laboratory and probably won't even come out for lunch.'

'I thought you were supposed to stay in bed for a few days,' Jancis reminded her.

'Phooey to that,' Sophie scoffed. 'Thorp said if I felt better I might get out of bed this afternoon. But since he'll have his nose stuck down some test tube all day, he'll never know what time I left my bed. It's a pity we came down in his car. I feel lost without my motor. He did it on purpose, of course.'

'Did he?' Jancis hadn't given the matter any thought, but it was obvious Sophie had been speculating.

'Oh yes. While you were packing I roused myself to suggest we left then, and you could follow in my car. I thought I was home and dry with the suggestion,' Sophie said blithely. 'I could see he didn't want you here any more than you wanted to come. So thought he'd jump at the idea, hoping you'd forget to follow. I knew you wouldn't, of course.'

'You did,' Jancis broke in, knowing Sophie didn't mean to rub it in when she said her uncle didn't want her here—

it was the truth, after all.

'The way I saw it you'd given your word. You don't break promises, do you, Jancy?' said Sophie, then went on, 'Anyway, Thorp, to my amazement, said no, that we'd wait for you, then let me know he was fully aware my car was insured for owner drive only.'

'It is!' Jancis squeaked, feeling pale as she recalled she had driven the Morgan away from the party.

'Not *you* too,' said Sophie, as though suspecting she was going to be as upright about it as Thorp. 'It was my father's idea. He had the insurance changed last month after I'd lent the car to a friend who failed to return it. He must have told Thorp about it before he and Mother went off.'

With the Morgan not being at Widefields Manor anyway, Jancis couldn't see the point, since she wouldn't again be driving it, of trying to get through to Sophie that she should at least have warned her about her insurance before sending her on her way. For the present she was only hoping Sophie hadn't got anything too outrageous buzzing around in her head for them to do that day. When Sophie departed she got out of bed, bathed, dressed in a sage green trouser suit and met her downstairs for breakfast.

It wasn't Mrs Hemmings who saw to it they had everything they required, but Carol, a happy-go-lucky girl who confirmed Sophie's worst suspicions when she asked her what there was to do locally.

'Not a lot,' answered Carol.

It was while they were munching their way through toast, talking about any subject which presented itself, that Sophie told Jancis Mrs Hemmings had given up nursing after being involved in a pile-up.

'Mrs Hemmings was driving and came through without a scratch,' she said, reaching for more toast, her dieting craze a thing of the past. 'But Mr Hemmings suffered dreadful injuries. Not only that,' she went on, 'but his confidence went after the accident, and he doesn't like to be far away from Mrs Hemmings now.'

'Oh, the poor man,' said Jancis sympathetically.

'Terrible, isn't it? Anyway,' Sophie continued, 'Mrs Hemmings packed up her nursing and wrote after the job here when Mrs Timmins, Thorp's housekeeper at the time, decided to leave when her arthritis got so bad. Mrs Timmins lives in one of Thorp's cottages in the village,' she sidetracked, before returning, 'The Hemmings have been with Thorp about two years now. And Mrs Hemmings is so grateful to Thorp for taking them on in the first place, when she must have been at the end of her rope, that she'll do anything for him—even,' she said, adding a light note to what had been a tragic story, 'to go as far as putting up with me. Mrs Timmins used to throw up her hands in horror at the mere mention of my name, so I believe.'

Breakfast over, Sophie suggested a walk to the village. 'We can go and study the notice board on the village hall. Who knows,' she said, without much conviction, 'there might be a rave-up going on there tonight.'

For no other reason than that anything orthodox was taboo in her book, she took Jancis through the back way out of the house, giving her an insight into the layout as they trooped through the kitchen, stopping to say hello to Mrs Hemmings on their way. Mrs Hemmings said she was pleased to see Sophie looking so much better, and, not looking at all conscience-twinged, Sophie replied that she felt fine.

Mr Hemmings was outside in his wheelchair. Wrapped up snugly in an overcoat, a thick woollen blanket over his knees, he was taking advantage of the January sunshine. He had a sketch pad on his knees, but as far as Jancy could see didn't appear to have started anything. Sophie introduced her to the man who, though otherwise wrapped up, was bareheaded and had a thatch of prematurely white hair. Like Mrs Hemmings, Jancis judged him to be in his late forties, just as she judged that today was not one of his good days.

Her heart went out to him. His eyes were dull and lifeless, and he seemed to her to be a man entirely without hope. Sophie was about to move away, when the impulse came on Jancis.

'We're going for a walk as far as the village,' she smiled at him. 'Would you like to come?'

For several seconds he seemed startled by her invitation, but any expression as far as she was concerned was better than the hopelessness of his expression before—that expression that looked every bit as though he was sitting there waiting to die.

'I'm too heavy for you to push,' he said gruffly.

'No, you're not,' she denied, looking at his cadaverous face. 'And anyway, there are two of us if we come to an incline.' She waited; it was suddenly of great importance that he wasn't left sitting there with his own unhappy thoughts. 'You're scared,' she teased him softly, having seen some sign of him coming to life at her invitation. 'You think Sophie and I will take you to the top of the hill and let go the handles. We won't, I promise.'

More life came to his face. 'I'll have to see what Peggy thinks.'

Jancis went to the kitchen door and told Mrs Hemmings what she wanted to do. Mrs Hemmings was looking doubtful as she went outside with her. 'Would you like to go, love?' she asked her husband gently.

'I could do with some tobacco,' he replied. And Jancis couldn't understand the tears that came into Mrs Hemmings' eyes until Mrs Hemmings told her, a couple of days later, that he had been so down lately, he had even lost interest in his pipe.

'We'll take good care of him,' Jancis whispered to her.

Then with Sophie pushing with a will while chattering nineteen to the dozen to her half of their new responsibility, the three of them headed down the drive. None of them noticed that Thorp Kingman had left his test tubes to collect something from one of the outbuildings, and was standing looking contemplatively at their departing backs.

CHAPTER FIVE

BECAUSE the village was farther away than Jancis had realised, they were late getting back to lunch. Whether Thorp had broken off work for his meal she neither knew nor cared.

It had been hard work pushing Mr Hemmings, there being an unending succession of minor rises that were unnoticeable when travelling by car, but when pushing a wheelchair each gradient seeming steeper than the last. Still, she didn't regret her impulsive offer. Sophie had rattled on ceaselessly to Mr Hemmings, in actual fact, after her initial spurt, putting more energy into her conversation than into giving a hand with the pushing. But Jancis had seen as they stopped outside the village hall, and the three of them looked at the notice board, that the dead look had gone from his eyes.

They returned Mr Hemmings to his wife on the stroke of half past one, and if his eyes weren't exactly sparkling, then they were a good deal brighter than they had been.

'Sorry we've been so long,' Jancis apologised.

'But we stopped and chatted for ages to a man tidying up the War Memorial,' finished Sophie, 'then we went and had a cup of coffee with old Mrs Timmins. She doesn't get out much, and Jancis made the coffee while me and Mr Hemmings cheered her up.'

It couldn't last, Jancis knew that, but the whole morning had gone by without Sophie plotting some scheme that was guaranteed to have her hairless.

'Do you know, Jancy,' she said, looking through the window of the drawing room, where they had moved to after lunch, 'for one of the few times in my life I feel

65

really good about something I've done.'

'You do?' enquired Jancis, wondering what was coming.

'Mmmm. When I heard you suggest we take Mr Hemmings with us this morning I thought you'd gone potty. But I really enjoyed it—even having coffee with Mrs Timmins. For the first time ever I felt as though someone really needed me.'

'Everybody needs you, Sophie,' Jancis told her lightly. 'You're a tonic to most people you come into contact with.'

'And a pain in the *derrière* to the others,' said Sophie, giving a laugh and coming to sit down opposite her. 'What do you think about the disco at the village hall tonight? Shall we go?'

Not at all keen, but thinking it might be an idea to get some of the excess energy out of Sophie's system rather than let it build up, Jancis answered, 'We can go if you like—though since you're still supposed to be a semi-invalid, I think you'd better check with your uncle first.'

Sophie didn't view the idea of having to ask permission for so small an event at all favourably, but after some minutes of humming and hawing she said she supposed she was right.

'I'll go and see him now,' she said, her mind made up.

'He's working,' Jancis thought to mention.

'Then it'll do him good to have a break,' said Sophie, never one to wait for anything.

Left to herself, Jancis thought she had better start making noises about returning to London. Sophie wouldn't like it, but since, her sleep caught up on, she now looked the picture of health, she couldn't very well accuse her of breaking her promise because the reason for her being here, to nurse her ailing friend, no longer existed.

And yet she felt an odd reluctance to go. She couldn't fathom why she should feel that way when after her brush with Thorp Kingman last night she had decided that another minute spent in his house would be a minute too long. That was until she thought over the insults he had heaped on her, and then she knew it was because she wanted full retribution, and full retribution was hardly likely to be achieved with her in London and him here.

It shook her that she should feel so revengeful, that sort of feeling never having been part of her make-up before. But recalling Sophie saying not too many hours ago, 'I could see he didn't want you here,' had her thinking she would love to stay just for the perverse pleasure of knowing he would be wishing her a hundred miles away each time he looked at her. Could she stay on in a house where she wasn't wanted, though? It didn't take much thinking about when the way he had been with her flew into her mind. Suddenly it was just too much that he could think he could say whatever he liked to her and get away with it. Her mind was made up: she was staying. And what was more, she was going to snatch at any chance, however small, to even up the score.

A look of determination crossed her face as she renewed her vow to make Thorp pay. A fighting light entered her eyes, and a smile of anticipation was on her lips when Sophie burst in on her.

'Do you believe in love at first sight?' she asked, her skin delicately flushed, her eyes shining.

Here we go, thought Jancis, having hastily to change the direction of her thoughts. 'No,' she answered. Her feelings for Shaw had grown quite rapidly, but they hadn't been instant.

'There's this assistant Thorp has working for him. He's been with him weeks and I never knew,' Sophie said softly as though she hadn't heard the negative reply. 'I asked Thorp if we could go tonight, and then this man appeared out of nowhere and I almost had to pinch myself, because I thought I was dreaming.'

'So he's coming with us tonight,' said Jancis, knowing

how quickly Sophie achieved results when she went into action.

But Sophie shook her head. 'He's barely aware of my existence—yet,' she said. 'I swear he would have looked straight through me if Thorp hadn't thought to introduce us.' Her face took on a dreamy expression.

'Thorp said you could go?' Jancis questioned.

'Go? Go where? Oh, to the disco. Yes, that's O.K. But he wants to see you privately first.'

'Wants to see me?' she exclaimed. 'What on earth for? He doesn't for a minute think I have to ask his permission to go out, does he?'

She never received a reply, because Sophie had disappeared into her own little world again.

Because Thorp himself was going out that night, dinner was to be early. Probably has a hot date with Aileen Forbes, Jancis thought, sourly thinking them a pair well matched. Miss Forbes didn't look as though she would see a joke either unless someone hit her over the head with it.

Why the thought should bring a slight frown to her forehead that he must be going steady, convinced as she was that Aileen Forbes was his date, she had no idea. What she did know was that she had no intention of seeking him out so he could see her privately before she and Sophie went off to the disco. If he wanted to see her, then he could jolly well come looking.

By the time they went down to dinner they were late, Sophie having delayed them by taking her time in dressing. Most likely still dreaming about the man she had seen once and believed herself in love with, Jancis thought. Sophie had come a little way down to earth and was more like the infectiously good-humoured person she had been before Cupid's arrow had struck.

They were too late to have a pre-dinner drink. Not that Jancis wanted one. She wanted as little time spent with Thorp Kingman in social chit-chat as possible, and she knew he felt the same. He didn't at any rate take them to task for not appearing until the first course was about to be served.

'Does Gareth Logan live in the village?' Sophie opened the mealtime conversation, addressing Thorp and going to the heart of what she wanted to know without delay. And on being informed that no, he didn't, but lived in the town of Todsbridge some eight miles away, she then fired several questions at him concerning—how long had Gareth worked for him, did he come every day, and the last question, coming casually as though it had no special significance, was he married?

Thorp's face was serious when he answered, nothing showing of whether he was aware of any particular interest she might have in his assistant, until he had cleared up her last question.

'No, he isn't married,' he told her. 'But if you're thinking of livening up what you might think of as his dull ordinary life, then don't. Gareth is a serious-minded young man, at the moment happy in the work he's doing and keen to learn more. He can well do without the sort of disruption I can envisage you wreaking on his orderly life.'

Sophie's face was a picture of innocence. 'I don't know how you can suggest I would do such a thing, Thorp! I just thought, since you say he's not married, that he might be a little lonely.' Thorp surveyed the openness of her face without comment, and she went on, 'It just occurred to me that if he did live locally then he could well be at the disco tonight and that—well, since I got the impression he might be lonely, Jancis and I could try and cheer him up.'

Thorp's expression altered and Jancis saw from the way his brows came down that he was not at all thrilled with the idea of either of them trying to cheer his assistant up. His eyes swung in her direction and finding herself under the scrutiny of that darkened look, she knew right then that it was her in particular he didn't want having anything to do with Gareth Logan.

What did he think she would do to him, for goodness' sake? Did he think her appetite so great that she had to attempt to seduce every man she came into contact with? She glowered back at him. One day, she thought—Oh yes, Thorp Kingman, one day!

'Whose idea was it to take Jack Hemmings with you when you went out this morning?'

Jancis felt there was nothing she wanted to say to him, so she left Sophie to do the answering. Though from the way Sophie was colouring, she gathered she was realising she had been caught out in not obeying Thorp's instruction that she keep to her room until after lunch. But Sophie being Sophie soon overcame any discomfort she might have been feeling, and after a quick look at Jancis, seeing it was being left up to her to reply, she gave Thorp a wicked grin and said:

'If we're going to get into trouble about it, then it was my idea.'

'Why should you get into trouble?' Thorp asked. 'When I saw Jack Hemmings this afternoon he was busily sketching away and in the best spirits I've seen him in for weeks.'

'Oh,' said Sophie, her grin widening, 'in that case, it was Jancy who asked him if he'd like to come with us.'

Jancis concentrated on her meal as Sophie conveyed this piece of information to Thorp, and the meal progressed with her having to add hardly anything to the conversation. Not that Thorp Kingman appeared to notice she had little to say. But by the time the meal was over and they left the table, far from not looking forward to going to the disco, she was now eager to get out of the house and release the tensions she had felt coiling up within her throughout the meal.

Out in the hall her only thought was to go up to her room for a coat to put over the camisole top dress she was wearing. But apparently Thorp had other ideas.

'I'd like a word, Jancis,' he said with every appearance of pleasantness.

But that was purely for Sophie's sake since, she was standing close by, Jancis knew that. Wondering if she should express the unladylike thought that was going through her head of 'Go and take a running jump', she looked at Sophie and realised it still wasn't too late, if she upset him, for him to revoke his permission for Sophie to go to the disco.

'Certainly,' she said in a civilised voice, and found she was being ushered into a room that must be his study since it housed a large oak desk, the top of which had papers plus smudges of dust here and there which she gathered meant Mrs Hemmings only touched his desk at her peril.

For several seconds after Thorp had closed the door on an inquisitive Sophie, he said nothing at all. He propped himself on the corner of the desk but didn't invite Jancis to sit down. From that she hoped this interview was going to be brief, as absently the thought came that dressed as he was in a dark suit and crisp white shirt, he was getting nearer and nearer to being good-looking all the time. For long moments he continued to look at her, his hard grey eyes going over her in her red dress that instead of clashing with her titian hair complemented it beautifully. Determined not to be the first to speak, a mulish look about her mouth, Jancis waited.

'It hasn't gone unnoticed by me,' Thorp began, his look severe, 'that no man is safe from you.'

As a direct attack, and she was under no illusions that they weren't skirmishing on the edge of another battle, he couldn't have bettered it.

'Full marks to you for being so observant,' she fired her first broadside, knowing she was facing one man at least who had had all the inoculations against what it was he thought she had that was so fatal to his sex.

He ignored her sarcasm. 'Had I not witnessed for myself in London in a very short space of time that you go man-hunting as though you have a personal need to add as many scalps to your belt in the quickest possible time, I . . .'

'Scalps!' she echoed, wondering whether to laugh, or—as the palm of her right hand was growing distinctly itchy—let it fly somewhere near his left ear.

'Do you have to try to ensnare every man you meet?'

'I don't have to try,' she said flippantly. 'It comes naturally.'

He ignored that, looking at her coldly and ticking off, 'Adrian Hayward was ready to lie down and let you walk all over him. I saw you myself enjoying the advances of the man who was kissing you while you were dancing.' Vance, of course, she thought, having no intention of explaining her reasons for not stopping him when he had kissed her neck. 'I saw with my own eyes the way you hotfooted it to one of the bedrooms. We both know what I saw in that bedroom—though my view of a half-naked man and you with your skirt up round your thighs was probably better than yours.'

'No doubt,' she said chillingly, vaguely recalling that the skirt of her dress had ridden up when Vance had pulled her on to the bed.

'But even that wasn't sufficient for you, was it? I left calling at your flat until the next morning mainly because I was fed up with the run-around Sophie was giving me, but more because if she'd been sampling that high-octane punch being served at the party I guessed I'd get less sense out of her even than usual. But when I did call what do I discover? You have an entirely different man sharing your bed. Then no sooner do you arrive here than you're charming your way into Jack Hemmings' life. I saw the three of you come back. The man was actually laughing!'

Jancis could have inserted at that point that Jack Hemmings' good humour had been purely because no one could be miserable around Sophie for long, and seeing in Mrs Timmins a fellow-sufferer, that lady being in continual pain from arthritis, had awakened in him a need to try and cheer someone else up. He had probably felt as good as Sophie had done after his efforts.

'So,' she said challengingly, 'we've established that I'm a thorough bad lot. Was that what you wanted to see me about?' Her tone was insolent and she knew it—knew too, from the narrowing of his eyes, that he didn't care very much at all for her tone. But she refused to back down. 'It seems a futile exercise to me,' she added loftily. 'You have all the evidence you need to my character, what's the point of . . .'

'I have, haven't I?' he stopped her. 'But since I don't believe in finalising my conclusions until there's no longer any doubt——' His scientific work would have taught him that if nothing else, she thought, clearly remembering that day long ago when she had broken his car headlamps. As livid as he had been then, he had thought to ask her first if she knew anything about it before he had laid into her. '—And since you haven't bothered to deny any of what we've been talking about——' He had the evidence of his eyes, was he saying he would have listened had she tried to defend herself? She didn't believe it for a second. And anyway, why should she want to defend herself *to him*? '—I'll tell you exactly what the point of this discussion is. Given the odd scandal or two common in most villages, the little community ticks over very well. You and Sophie will be enjoying very shortly some of the entertainment the village provides. I regret that it's necessary for me to tell you to make sure the only entertainment you enjoy is that to be found within the confines of the Village Hall.'

Jancis' eyebrows shot up. Flabbergasted, she stared at

him. 'You mean . . .' she gasped, sure she must have mis-construed his meaning.

'I mean,' he told her bluntly, entirely unimpressed that she was looking staggered, 'that when tea is brought to your room early tomorrow morning, I don't want any of my staff to find a stray tomcat in your bed.'

Which came first, her shriek of outrage or the lightning-quick movement of her hand, she couldn't have said. Both came without her volition, so perhaps they came together. But the crack of her hand as it caught Thorp a stinging blow to the side of his face brought her awake to what she had done. And then there was no time for thought, for after the briefest moment when shock registered in Thorp's face before it changed into fury, the blow she had struck him being entirely unexpected, he had hauled her into his arms, and his mouth was punishing hers in a brutal kiss.

If she was furious, then he was incensed, and her effort to get free, which was mighty, was harnessed without any trouble as he refused to let her go, his arms like steel bonds around her.

Ruthlessly he kissed her, his mouth grinding her lips against her teeth, his body rigid against hers crushing her breasts up against him. Even when he broke his kiss to stare down into her wide green eyes, he didn't let go of her but grated:

'You think you can get away with throwing your weight around that adolescent herd you run with, but don't try it with me, girl. Hit me and I hit back!'

Only he didn't hit her, but brought his mouth into contact with hers again. But this time his initial aggression was missing and instead of kissing her as a punishment, he was less violent, his mouth softer, warmer. Jancis had no intention of kissing him back, that was the last thing she had in mind.

Why then did her mouth soften too? She didn't know. His grip was still firm, but less like steel, and strangely her struggles were less vigorous than they had been. When, with an expertise she found shattering, his lips had hers parting, she was too bemused to be aware of it.

What she was aware of was that she had never thought the man she had dubbed as a miserable stuffed shirt, a man totally lacking in humour, could kiss this way. Strange exciting feelings began to make themselves felt in her body. She mustn't feel like this, she mustn't, she tried to think. But as his mouth left hers to seek unsuspected pulse spots in her throat, by her ear, her legs began to go weak.

She was clutching on to him by the time the exquisite touch of his mouth settled once more on hers. She wanted to press her body nearer to his as her lips parted voluntarily, and found she was doing just that, the whole length of her body moulding to his in sheer enjoyable sensation that she knew he was feeling too as his mouth plundered hers.

Only he couldn't have been feeling the same as her, she realised a moment later. For without any effort, it seemed, Thorp was suddenly pushing her away. Her eyes flickered open, her senses bewildered. She thought she caught a glimpse of warmth in his eyes, but in the blink of an eye that warmth had disappeared as ice sent it on its way.

'I did say no man is safe from you, I believe,' he told her coolly; his control, she saw, had never for a moment wavered. 'Perhaps I should qualify that and say that if you have any ideas of playing nearer to home, I just don't turn on for women like you.' He paused long enough to take in that her colour was still high. 'Might I suggest you stay in my study while you cool down if you don't want Sophie to know you're feeling sore that your advances have been rejected.'

Had he stayed a moment longer, Jancis wasn't sure her already haywire senses wouldn't have had her taking another swing at him. Absolutely livid, her legs weak—though she wasn't sure whether that was because a man she thought so hateful could have aroused her sexual awareness so that she had no idea what she was doing, had acted on instinct alone, or whether it was her fury that made her legs feel weak—she sat down in the nearest chair to hand.

Minutes went by as she silently called him every name she could lay her tongue to. She then spent another five minutes in further castigation of him. Her advances? He had grabbed her! Did he think she always led up to a hectic love scene by inviting being kissed by taking a swipe at the man she was interested in? Her hand still stung from that blow.

A further five minutes and a deep hatred entered her heart for the man who had trampled her pride. She had gone over again all the things she would like to do to him, boiling in oil being mild by comparison. Among her many outraged thoughts was the one of packing her bags right this minute. She did in fact half rise from her chair to go and do just that, then sat down again. She wanted her revenge on that swine, and she was hardly likely to get that if she put herself out of his orbit. Again she renewed her vow; she'd stay on here if it killed her. Stay, and at every opportunity, make him pay.

As she realised she must have been sitting there for all of fifteen minutes, her anger was spurred yet again that if Thorp Kingman had not yet gone out, then he must be patting himself on the back that his kisses had so electrified her that she was taking all this time to cool down.

In a second she had the study door open and was up the stairs in a flash, and it was there Sophie found her not long afterwards.

'Thorp has just gone out,' she said, coming into the room. 'Ready?'

'I just have to put my coat on.'

Sophie had borrowed a torch from Mrs Hemmings because parts of the road they would be going along were unlighted. 'Thorp said he would give us a lift if we were ready to go now,' she said as they walked along. 'But I thought if you'd been fighting with him you wouldn't fancy that much, so I refused.' They trudged a few more steps. 'Were you fighting with him?' she asked.

'Now why should I fight with him?' Jancis had no intention of telling a soul what had taken place in that study, but she needed time to think up something that would cover what Thorp had wanted to see her about.

'I don't know,' observed Sophie, 'but it seems to me every time I look at you and Thorp together that there's static in the air.'

'We didn't fight,' said Jancis, trying to keep her feelings about what had happened out of her voice, and knowing Sophie was going to ask if she didn't tell her. 'Actually your uncle wanted to know if you were really fit to go to this disco. Er—he asked me to look after you.'

'Did he really?' asked Sophie, who hadn't thought she had fooled him about being ill. Then, her affection for him showing, she said softly, 'Bless him.'

Bless him! He'd need to be blessed if she had her way, Jancis thought with silent indignation.

She didn't even get to put her nose inside the Village Hall. She went up the two steps with Sophie, who then opened the door to go through, then stood transfixed, blocking the door, before hastily closing it.

'Don't go in there,' she said in horrified tones as though she had just seen a dead body. Jancis followed her away from the hall, where Sophie promptly leaned up against a nearby wall and started to laugh.

'So much for our rave-up, Jancy,' she giggled. 'If any one of those kids in there is above sixteen, I'll eat my Sunday best!' Her laughter subsided, and never short on ideas, she straightened away from the wall. 'Come on, let's go and see what the village pub has to offer.'

The Red Lion offered nothing. Apart from two elderly

men sitting in one corner who looked to be permanent
fixtures, the pub was deserted. 'Mine's all right,' whispered Sophie, smiling at the two old men, 'but I don't
much like the look of yours.'

Only just managing to keep her face straight, not
wanting the two regulars to know since Sophie had been
looking at them that her remark had been about them
and had tickled her, Jancis went with Sophie to order
their drinks.

'Darts night,' explained the landlord, when Sophie
suggested that perhaps bubonic plague was going around,
only word hadn't reached the Manor yet. 'The team are
playing an away match, and taken my trade with them as
supporters.'

Sophie kept up a more or less one-sided flow of talk
while they sipped their shandies, while Jancis tried to
concentrate not to let her attention wander. But the feel
of Thorp's arms around her, the shock of knowing she
had responded to such a vile creature, broke her concentration time and time again.

Maybe Sophie sensed that she wasn't quite with her,
for before either of them were half way down their drinks,
she was suggesting that, there being nothing else to do in
the village of Abbotts Hanley, which she had already
nicknamed 'the last outpost', they might as well return to
the Manor and see if there was anything worthwhile
watching on the box.

Jancis made a determined effort to keep Thorp
Kingman out of her thoughts as they retraced their steps.
She found it hard going as she and Sophie sat watching a
comedy series on television she had always before found
hilarious, but tonight, for some reason, didn't seem funny
at all.

Sophie didn't seem to think it funny either, for she got
up and flicked round to the different channels. This alone
brought Jancis's mind away from the scene in the study

to wonder what truth there was in her friend's assertion that she had fallen instantly in love with Gareth Logan, for Sophie liked to laugh above all else.

'I think I'll go to bed,' said Sophie, leaving the set switched on just as the announcer introduced the final episode of a spy thriller William had been hooked on.

William seemed so far away. He'd be delighted to know who the 'mole' was, Jancis thought. She could stay and watch. It would be ages before Thorp Kingman came home, she'd be in bed long before then.

'William was following this serial,' she told Sophie. 'I'll stay down and watch, then I can write and tell him how it ended.'

After receiving her assurance that there was no need for her to stay down too, Sophie went off, leaving her to it. But for all her good intentions, having not been following the complicated plot as closely as her brother, within five minutes Jancis found her attention wandering.

What was Thorp Kingman doing now? she caught herself out thinking, and immediately turned her attention back to the set. She wasn't at all interested in anything that man did. I'll bet any money he's with that snooty Aileen Forbes, her attention drifted again. Well, she was welcome to him.

A yawn escaped her and she leaned her head back against the soft upholstery of the settee. Her vision went hazy and she blinked to keep awake. Without being aware of it she lifted her feet on to the settee, adjusting her position to make herself comfortable.

She had been asleep over an hour when the front door opened. She was oblivious to the fact that someone had entered the room, taken in her sleeping form, her face half buried in a cloud of titian hair. She had no idea Thorp Kingman had gone to switch the television off before coming to stand and look down at her for a few seconds prior to reaching down his arms to her.

CHAPTER SIX

JANCIS came through a long tunnel of a deep sleep to find herself on the settee and that her host had his arms around her. Still only half awake, strangely, maybe perhaps he was looking at her for the first time without that familiar ice in his eyes, she didn't panic.

His eyes had a warm look to them, she thought, and as she remembered his lips on hers, her eyes went to his mouth as his head came nearer.

'Don't kiss me,' she whispered insanely, feeling at home in his arms, when had she been fully awake she would have vigorously fought her way out of them.

'I wasn't going to,' he told her quietly, nothing urgent or harsh in his look. 'You don't look too comfortable there, my idea was to carry you to your room so you could finish off your sleep in comfort.'

'Oh,' she said softly, the mists of sleep refusing to clear since he was being so much less brutal with her.

'Why don't you want me to kiss you?' he asked, nothing about him hurried. 'You enjoyed my kissing you before.'

'You've been kissing her,' she said, quite without thought. Then at his reminding her of that other kiss, the way he had pushed her away, and the fury that had engulfed her afterwards, she went a fiery red and came to full wakefulness.

Hastily, too hastily, she pushed his arms from her and was on her feet before she had her sea legs. Thorp had risen too, and his arms came round her, this time refusing to let her go when it looked as though her legs weren't going to hold her.

'So it offends your sense of decency to have a man come

80

to you straight from having someone else in his arms?' he enquired. And if she had thought she had witnessed a more gentle side to his nature than he had up to now shown her, then Jancis knew she could forget it. For that harsh note was back again when he said, 'It's a pity it doesn't work in reverse, isn't it?'

She tried to pull out of his arms at that, but he wouldn't let her go. She knew full well he was referring to what he thought had gone on between her and Vance, and very shortly after, Davy. Perhaps she wasn't as fully awake as she thought, because it had never been in her mind to defend herself against him. But when only a few hours ago nothing would have had her aiming for his good opinion, she found herself trying to tell him:

'Davy didn't . . .' only she didn't get any farther, because he was cynically interrupting her.

'You're not going to tell me he didn't sleep in your bed?'

His tone said he wasn't going to believe her even if she was. From the evidence of his own ears he had heard Davy thank her for the use of her bed. He wasn't to know she had slept in William's bed.

'Well, he did, but . . .'

Apparently, Thorp wasn't ready to hear any more. His lip curled as though she sickened him, and he put her roughly away from him.

'Oh, go to bed!' he snapped dismissively, and the arrogance in him infuriated her.

Who did he think he was, to dismiss her as if she was some little scrubber? Then when she hadn't moved, but stood there glaring at him, he added insult to injury.

'Do I take it the disco didn't yield anything and that you don't like to go to bed hungry?'

Oh, the sarcastic swine! If he hadn't casually strolled over to the drinks tray and begun pouring himself a Scotch, had he still been within slapping distance, she was furious enough to chance her arm a second time.

He turned, glass in hand, and looked down at her from the length of his nose as though surprised to see her still there.

'What are you waiting for?' he asked tautly. 'Is it that far from not wanting me to kiss you, you were in fact bringing something sexual into the air where I can assure you as far as I was concerned none existed?'

'You . . .' She searched for a word that was vile enough for him, only to find he wasn't waiting while she searched through words not in common usage, not by her at any rate.

'Forget it,' he said, taking a swig of his whisky. 'I kissed you once in punishment. To kiss you a second time would be a punishment for me.'

'You pompous, conceited prig!' split the air as her temper exploded, there being no need now to look for choice words as fury spilled from her. 'I don't know who you think you are, but let me tell you that never have I met such a pedantic, pragmatical, smug, overbearing swine as you!' The words kept coming, she couldn't have stopped them if she tried, and she had no intention of trying. 'You might think I'm not good enough to breathe the same saintly air as you, but at least I know how to laugh!' Gulping for breath, she raged on, 'My God, it's a wonder you haven't got a permanent headache, your halo's stuck on so tight. It's about time you came out of your stuffy corner and looked about you, though to save you the shock, I'll tell you—we're living in the 1980s now, not the last century.'

Her cheeks flaming, she came to a halt to see she hadn't even dented the surface of him. He was surveying her coolly; her tirade had obviously not affected him one iota. That he hadn't attempted to interrupt her once she got started was, she had hoped, because he was shattered to hear so many home truths being flung at him. But he didn't look shattered, she had to own, and she had nothing else she could think of to fling at him. She moved to the door, sure she would come up with a hundred much better, much more cutting things she could have fired at him later.

She turned when she reached the door. For the moment she had run out of steam, or thought she had, until one look at the indifferent way he was looking at her added fuel to her boiler.

'And as for letting you kiss me again,' she threw at him, her hand on the door handle, 'I'm more fussy who I kiss than you think. The only reason I kissed you back was because I was intrigued to know just how far a strait-laced misery like you would go!'

She waited, only to see his eyes narrow at that remark, knew at last she had got to him, then was through the door and racing to her room.

Victory was hers, she was thinking delightedly an hour later. She had definitely jarred him with that last stab. Sitting up in bed, the bedside lamp on, she was much too pleased with herself to think of going to sleep. She hadn't heard Thorp come up the stairs and she sincerely hoped he was where she had left him, taking stock of his character. If her words had had the effect on him she hoped, then she wouldn't be surprised if he finished off the whole bottle of Scotch when he realised what a miserable creature he was.

She had never willingly hurt a soul in her life, but he'd had it coming. Oh yes, he'd had it coming. Who did he think he was that he could say what he liked to her and get away with it, for goodness' sake?'

Feeling as though the score card was just a shade more even, she heard his footsteps on the stairs. They passed her room without hesitation. They were neither staggered nor lurching, so he couldn't have hit the bottle after all. Jancis' sense of satisfaction waned, as the unwanted thought penetrated, with a ring of truth to it, that she hadn't so much as pricked the surface of him.

Damn, she thought, she had been so certain when she had seen his eyes narrow that she had struck a chord of recognition of his own shortcomings. She had been positive when she had called him a strait-laced misery that she had got him. Well, if he thought she was going to apologise, he could whistle!

Not anywhere near as elated as she had been, she sat there for another ten minutes. Her spirits had dipped lower to be positively basement level before she came to the conclusion that the score card was very much the same as it had been. Thorp had stayed cool when she had let fly with her temper and she had gained nothing at all, only adding 'shrieking shrew' to the other things he thought her. Not that she was going to do anything to change his opinion. She had tried to tell him about Davy and look what had happened. She had lost her temper, used up all her ammunition—the next round had to be his.

Her thoughts vanished into nothing as her ears picked up a sound outside her door, and her eyes flew wide as she saw the door handle turn. Then the door was pushed inwards, and her heart started to race as Thorp, dressed only in pyjama bottoms, came silently into her room, and just as silently closed the door behind him.

She tried to find her voice, but her vocal cords seemed paralysed as she just sat and stared at him. His shoulders were broad, magnificent she might have thought if she wasn't too frightened to think at all, and his chest was shadowed with dark hair. He's only come to frighten me, she made herself think as he moved forward. He had a tenacious look of purpose about him that had her remembering that jibe she had flung at him that she'd only kissed him back because she had wanted to see how far he would go. Had he come to show her just how *far* he *would* go? asked an inner, disturbed voice. Surely not? No, not Thorp. He wouldn't, she argued inwardly as her disturbed feelings grew larger. Oh lord, he thought there were no limits she set herself, she thought, a definite feeling of anxiety starting up. He looked so powerful, strong muscles

showing in his uncovered arms—she wouldn't stand a
chance! Then he had reached the bed, was staring as
though fascinated at her creamy shoulders exposed by her
flimsy nightdress.

'I . . .' she croaked, cowardly wondering if an apology
would satisfy him.

'I,' he said, 'have been thinking about what you said,
Jancis.' He was near enough for her to smell whisky on
his breath. Oh God, he's drunk, she thought, he doesn't
know what he's doing. 'You said,' he reminded her, 'that
it was about time I came out of my stuffy corner and into
the 1980s.'

Oh, how she wished she hadn't. She didn't trust that
gleaming light in his eyes. 'Yes, but . . .' she tried.

'You said I was a strait-laced misery,' he recalled, and
she knew he was drunk when he said, 'I thought I'd better
do something about that,' for the man she judged him to
be would never, sober, have done what he did next. For
while the saliva dried in her mouth so that not so much as
a scream would leave her throat, he had flipped back the
covers and moved. And in the stunned terrible moment
that followed, she heard him add, 'Let's see just exactly
how fussy you are, my dear,' and then they were both
under the covers, both in the same bed.

It was when Thorp made a grab for her that Jancis
moved—in the opposite direction. His hands never touched
her. Instead of his arms coming round her as she saw was his
intent, all he grabbed was the air as, caught off balance, he
fell forward and lay face down in the pillows.

She thought she saw his shoulders shake, but she wasn't
waiting to see if the alcohol he had consumed had brought on
a convulsion. In a flash she was at the door, throwing a hasty
glance backwards at his now still form, his face hidden. From
his still body she knew he had passed out. Compressing her
lips, she was through the door and was on the landing
outside, her only covering her flimsy nightdress.

Well, it was for sure she wasn't going back into that room until he had gone. It crossed her mind to go and ask Sophie if she could kip in with her. She had in fact taken two steps in that direction before it hit her how fond Sophie was of Thorp. If she went and woke her up she would have to tell her that her uncle turned amorous when he'd had a few and that even a guest beneath his roof wasn't safe from him.

Put out, she turned towards the stairs, thinking she might as well go and make herself comfortable on the settee. The state Thorp was in, he'd never make it down the stairs, not on two feet he wouldn't.

Muttering a few unpleasant thoughts about her host, Jancis sat down on a settee in the drawing room. It had come as a bit of a surprise to discover that Thorp could let go sufficiently at times and hit the bottle, though she hardly thought, on reflection, that what she had said had driven him to it. He *must* be drunk, she reasoned; sober he would never have come to her room.

She hugged her bare arms around her, feeling a chill in the room since the central heating had automatically cut out and probably wouldn't switch itself on again until about six o'clock. Shivering, she recalled one of the revellers at a party she had gone to one time passing out cold like that after drinking too freely. She could see his face though she couldn't recall his name, but somebody had put him to bed and she had been told he hadn't remembered a thing about it when he had awakened the next morning.

The cold began to bite into her scantily clad form, and her resentment grew that Thorp Kingman was tucked up snugly in her bed while she sat there probably catching pneumonia. Perhaps he had come to and staggered back to his room, she thought, without too much hope.

Half an hour later, when she was sure she was blue with cold, her resentment of Thorp Kingman had turned into a constructive force, and her bare feet were taking her silently up the stairs.

She had thought her intention was to go into the room and pluck her cuddly warm dressing gown from off the bottom of the bed where she had left it. But on entering the room, the table lamp still glowing the way it had been when she had so hastily departed, she tiptoed nearer to the bed and saw Thorp had turned his back to the light and was still out cold.

The idea of evening up the score card, and more than that, coming out of this with a massive debit on his side, was on her before she knew it. Dared she do it, though? Her spirit, never down for very long, reasoned against the good sense of what she was about to do. She owed him, didn't she? And anyway, how could she deprive herself of seeing his stunned, mortified face when he came to in the morning? Oh no, she just couldn't miss this opportunity. She would hate herself for evermore if she did. Thorp Kingman, with his high regard for good manners, his rigid sense of right and wrong, was going to receive the shock of his life when he woke up and found himself in bed with her.

Silently she crept back to the door and noiselessly closed it. Then, taking the utmost care not to wake him, she went back to the bed and very gently lifted the covers on the side away from him, and hardly daring to breathe, slid beneath them.

While waiting for sleep to come she sought round for the perfect phrase to greet him with. A smile of pure pleasure flitted across her face as she found it. She thought, 'Hello tomcat,' couldn't have been more perfect. Oh, he'd go puce with remorse, she thought with delight, and was hard put to it to stifle a chuckle.

Jancis drifted up from sleep feeling snug and warm and went to turn over. Something solid was in the way. She'd disturbed it. It moved! Her eyes flew wide to see dawn was about to break, but that not only had she left the lamp on, but she was in bed with Thorp, who was now awake and moving into a sitting position.

He stared at her, his eyes showing amazement, and at his amazed look all thoughts of how she was going to greet him disappeared, and the idea that had come to her about two o'clock that morning now seemed terrible in the extreme.

'I . . .' she began, and found she was blushing furiously. Her nightdress had slipped from one shoulder and she saw his dazed look rest there before moving down to what he could see of the swell of her breast.

'What the hell . . .?' ripped from him at the same time.

Her glance flitted from his face to that broad naked chest so near, and she began to tremble. How the heck was she going to get out of this one? Then she saw in his face a look that told her he was putting his own interpretation on what they were doing in the bed together. And she knew precisely at that moment that she wasn't going to explain, not the truth anyway. For it was as plain as day that although Thorp had no recollection of how he came to be in her bed, he was of the opinion that he had been welcomed. And it made her mad, made her furious that he was always so ready to blame her for everything. Tearing her eyes away from his face, not wanting him to see she was fuming, she turned to bury her head in her pillow.

'How could you?' she wailed accusingly, just loud enough for him to hear. 'Oh, how could you?'

There was a dumbfounded silence, as she had expected. Then his voice, sounding a shade puzzled—well, she'd expected that too—'How could I—what?'

'You—don't even—remember, do you?' she moaned, in no hurry to answer his question; he didn't deserve any better. 'You were too drunk to remember.'

'I wasn't drunk,' he protested, his voice taking on that harsh note she was familiar with and spurring her resolve to make him cringe. The lying devil! He had been as drunk as a skunk.

'You wouldn't have done what you did to me had you been sober,' she sighed, and only just stifled a scream of fright as his hands came down on either shoulder and he turned her so he could see into her face.

It took all her acting ability, and then some, to keep the blaze of fury from showing in her face, but she thought she managed it as she lay there with her glorious hair spread out across the pillow, though she dared not meet his eyes, unsure that her own weren't sparking her fury.

The harsh note had disappeared when Thorp next spoke, and his voice was very cool when he asked, 'Perhaps you wouldn't mind telling me just what it was I did do?'

Jancis looked at him then and saw the shock of waking up and finding himself in bed with her had gone from him. He was now taking the whole matter much too calmly for her liking. According to her reckoning, he should by now be on his knees grovelling for her forgiveness.

It was with the intention of again shocking him out of that calmness that she let her head roll to one side, made her voice sound dull and flat, with just about the right amount of pathos in it, she thought, as she stammered:

'I . . . I was a v-virgin until you came to my room last night.' Her groan, she thought, was a nice touch, before she added accusingly, 'Oh, how could you?' She wished she had Sophie's capacity to cry at will, but failing that she closed her eyes, not wanting Thorp to see their expression when he grovelled his apology.

'I think the question of your virginity before my arrival is a moot point,' he said, not grovelling at all, and almost having her opening her eyes to spit fury at him. Then bluntly he was asking, 'Are you trying to tell me that in a drunken state I came to your room and made love to you? Because if you are, let me tell you . . .'

Jancis didn't allow him to finish. 'I thought better of you, Thorp,' she snapped, feeling strangely insulted that he was as good as saying that drunk or sober he would never fancy her. That he could never imagine himself taking her, that even while so drunk he couldn't remember what had happened he just knew he wouldn't have touched her.

Her fury died, leaving her feeling slightly sick. 'I think you'd better go,' she said flatly. 'Sophie might take it into her head to pop in—she did yesterday morning. And if it isn't Sophie, you wouldn't want Carol finding you in your guest's bed when she brings the tea up, would you?'

Perhaps if he had stayed, questioned her further, she might have relented, confessed that nothing had happened between them. But he didn't stay. Without another word, though he did give another look at her, he got out of bed and went from the room. And her anger returned full force. It wasn't the slightest bit of good telling herself that he had been right to go. That in order to keep Sophie under control he had to show her a good example, or that when Carol brought the tea the goings-on at the Manor might be all over the village before the day was out.

When she went down to breakfast, Jancis was still feeling aggrieved that Thorp had left her as though, if he had to be caught in bed with someone, then from choice she would be the last person he would select. Not that she wanted to go to bed with him. Good grief, he'd be the last person she would choose either. But . . .

'You're very quiet,' said Sophie, who had been late getting up and was just coming round. 'Anything the matter?'

About to say, 'Look, Sophie, would you mind if I went home,' she never asked the question, because the door opened and Thorp came in. He said a general 'Good morning' which covered Jancis as well as Sophie, answered unruffled Sophie's pert question of what was he doing taking his nose off the grindstone when it was only ten to nine, then addressed Jancis direct.

'Could you come and see me in my study when you've finished your breakfast, Jancis?' he asked, quite pleasantly, she thought, though she knew any pleasantness for her was solely because Sophie was there, her ears cocked.

'Yes,' she assented briefly, and turned her attention to her coffee, her colour high as he went out.

'Goody,' said Sophie, not noticing Jancis' heightened colour as her brain began to plan. 'Try and keep him as long as you can, it'll give me a chance to nip round to the laboratory and have Gareth to myself.' She accepted the coffee Jancis had poured for her and looking up, noticed how pale she had suddenly turned.

'I say!' she exclaimed. 'You're not worried about seeing Thorp, are you?' And forgetting Gareth for a moment, 'I'd come with you, only if Thorp wants to see you in his study he means he wants to be private and he'd tip me out.'

'No, I'm not worried,' said Jancis, giving serious thought to not going at all. She was growing to dislike Thorp more by the hour.

'Any idea what he wants to talk to you about?' Sophie asked, adding, 'You know, this could become a habit. You were having a cosy chat with him in the study before we went out last night.' Her eyes brightened suddenly. 'I say, you two aren't . . .'

'No, we're not,' Jancis said sharply.

'Sorry I spoke,' Sophie said with a grin, then, thoughtfully, 'He's not bad-looking, you know, Jancy. He's only thirty-seven, too. Just the right age for you. Hey, what if . . .'

'Stop right there, Sophie,' Jancis ordered severely, doubly sure now she would be going back to London that day, for it looked as though without any other devilry

Sophie could get up to, she was now ready to try her hand at matchmaking.

'Pity,' said Sophie. 'I'd have liked you for an aunt.' Then before Jancis could broach the subject of leaving, Sophie was putting down her cup. 'Will you excuse me if I dash off? I'd like to pop up to my room and change before I go and see Gareth.' She went, taking Jancis' excusing her as read, which left Jancis on her own to consider if she was interested in complying with Thorp's wish to see her in his study.

She had had time since his departure from her room to wonder if she had been totally wrong in assuming he was stoned to the point of amnesia. She had been so certain before. But if he had not been near paralytic, then she had no answer to why he had come to her room in the first place. He had reminded her that she had called him a strait-laced misery, had said too, 'I thought I'd better do something about that,' before she had evaded the grab he had made for her. But surely he wouldn't have done that unless he had been tanked up?

Yet the more she thought about it the more she came round to the view that she had been wrong to think him inebriated. Though she was puzzled to find any other explanation for his behaviour. Had he possessed anything approaching a sense of humour she could have put it down to some devilry in him that had prompted him to jolt her out of the conviction she had of him being a strait-laced misery. But he didn't have a sense of humour, she was certain about that.

She was certain, too, that she knew why he wanted to see her in his study. He wanted to know what the hell she thought she was playing at by accusing him of having had his 'wicked way' with her, and no doubt about it, she was in for a verbal thrashing.

She supposed she should thank him that he intended to do that in private, and, never one to shirk taking her medicine, she knew she was going to face him. Though she had no intention of facing him with her tail between her legs. She left the breakfast room and made for the study with her chin held high. She only hoped that when their set-to was over—for she couldn't see herself taking all Thorp had to say quietly—she had got in first and said she was leaving, before he had the chance to tell her he was throwing her out.

CHAPTER SEVEN

IT didn't help Jancis' mutinous thoughts that she was left cooling her heels for a few minutes when she arrived in the study. Since he was expecting her she hadn't bothered to knock on the study door, but had gone straight in, only to find it empty.

She had her back to the room and was looking out of the window, telling herself if he didn't show within the next minute then that was that, she was going straight to her room to pack. And then she heard the door being opened and closed, and tensed momentarily before, her face composed, she turned to see Thorp standing by the door, his face as expressionless as she hoped hers was.

'You finished breakfast sooner than I thought,' he said, ignoring the chair behind the desk and going to one of the two softer-looking ones near to where she was standing by the window. 'Sit down, Jancis,' he said, and she felt his control, his authority, as he made his order sound like a suggestion. 'We might as well be comfortable,' he added.

He remained standing until he had seen her seated, then still in the same cool voice, he said, just in case she was in any doubt what he wanted to speak to her about, 'We had to leave our discussion half way, earlier this morning. Perhaps now you'll tell me exactly what it is you're trying to pull.'

'Trying to pull?' she echoed, the distasteful idea crossing her mind that he thought her idea in joining him back in that bed last night was in order that she could blackmail him in some way. The thought did her temper no good at all. 'I'm trying to pull nothing,' she snapped, and hated that he could look so calm when she was fast losing control. 'And stop trying to put me in the wrong! I didn't invite you to my room last night—you came without the slightest encouragement from me. I didn't ask you to stay either,' she added for good measure.

If anyone was going to be made to feel guilty, then it certainly wasn't going to be her. Even if she could now see she had been wrong to get back into that bed again, her plan to have Thorp grovelling having gone up in smoke.

'So,' he said, after a few moments' thought, 'you're maintaining that after I came to your room I seized hold of you and—what? Seduced you? Raped you?'

To her startled ears it sounded very much as though his memory failed him after he had come into her room.

'Don't you remember?' she dared, having no concrete plan in mind now, but still sufficiently angry to want to see him feel a little discomfited.

'I remember coming to your room. Remember lying on your bed. But . . .' his gaze flicked over her before he turned his attention to the window, 'but the rest is a blank. I can't remember a thing after that until I felt your elbow digging me in the back this morning.'

Got him! she thought elatedly, thoroughly looking forward to the next few minutes. Oh, the glory to be found in making him feel as small as countless times he had tried to make her feel!

'I see,' she said slowly, and almost burst out laughing when she saw his gaze still on something out of the window, and it dawned on her that he was too ashamed to look at her.

'Was it rape, Jancis?' he asked quietly.

Wanting badly to say yes, wanting to watch him shrivel up inside, for whatever else she thought about him, instinct told her that to believe he had raped a woman would shake him to the very foundations, she found she couldn't. Even if she only let him believe it for as long as this interview took, the affirmative answer just wouldn't leave her. And curse as she might that something in her refused to release the word, she told him, looking down at her lap:

'It started out that way, but . . .'

'But your sexual appetite got the better of you,' he inserted.

If there had been any sign of weakening in her resolve to get even with him, then he couldn't have said anything better to strengthen her need to make him pay, not only for that but for previous slighting remarks as well.

'Perhaps,' she said, her head coming up so she could look at him, sparks flaring in her green eyes for all she tried to douse them. 'You were too experienced for me,' she explained, her voice low. 'I—I didn't stand a chance.' She broke off, a brilliant thought coming into her head so that she had to look down again, much as she would like to have seen his reaction. 'Oh God,' she said painfully, 'what if I'm pregnant?'

'*Pregnant!*' The word exploded from him. He sounded so shaken that she just had to look at him regardless of whether he saw the triumph in her face that she had jolted him.

But it was she who received the jolt, for when she looked at that arrogant face, it looked momentarily as though he was about to laugh. Then she knew herself mistaken, because while she sat and watched, a terrible stillness came over him. She even thought he lost some of his colour, but thought herself mistaken in that too, as he stared hard at her, and grated harshly:

'So that's your game! You've got yourself into trouble and are looking for a father for your child.'

Red lights flashed as her temper went completely out of control. With a lightning movement she was out of her chair, his cutting remark another indication of the contempt he held her in, another indictment of what he thought her character. Her control had gone and she knew she would have lashed out at him.

But Thorp was out of his chair too, his hands pinning hers down to her sides, his voice soothing when he could see from her face how wrong he was. 'I'm sorry,' he apologised with charm she hadn't expected. 'Will you forgive me and put it down to the shock I received on hearing I may have fathered a child whose conception I have no remembrance of?'

His apology cooled her temper. But she would never forgive him for thinking what he had, even in shock.

'Perhaps I over-reacted,' she said, feeling his hands still hard on her arms, her temper under control, but only just. 'I told you this morning I—hadn't known a man before. I suppose I was in shock too that if I *am* pregnant you intend to deny paternity.'

Having never acted before, unless you could count being a fairy in a school play, Jancis, for all she had been telling the truth about never having been with a man, had no idea if Thorp was anywhere near to being taken in. But when he firmly though not ungently put her to sit back into the seat that only a minute before she had rocketed from, her spirit of hope was soaring upwards. He deserved every lie she could think of!

Thorp had returned to his seat too, but was leaning forward, his face serious. 'If what you say is true, Jancis,' he said slowly, his grey eyes having a hypnotic effect on her, making it impossible for her to look away, 'then some of the conclusions I've reached about you have been very wide of the mark.' His mouth took on a grim line. 'I think for a start you'd better tell me what you were doing when I saw that Lothario getting all the "yes" signals he needed from you at that party.'

With his direct look holding her, she felt a momentary twinge of alarm that no lies would come. Then the thought came that this part, the part where she had no need to lie to him, might possibly be more believable if she stuck to the truth. Fantastic as it would probably sound, she began:

'I think you already know that Adrian Hayward—er—thinks he's in love with me. Well, I told him as plainly as I could that I didn't love him. But that didn't stop him following me around and asking me to marry him, and he just wouldn't take no for an answer.'

That this appeared to have very little to do with the fact that she had tripped up the stairs with Vance Kettering taking the same route not so long afterwards didn't seem to fog Thorp following her, she thought, for he sat patiently listening.

'Go on,' he prompted. 'I could see for myself that the sun sets and rises with you for Adrian Hayward.' Whether he thought Adrian wanted his head seeing to for the way he felt about her, she couldn't judge.

'Well,' she said, 'I was in the middle of dancing with Vance Kettering, doing all I could to keep him at arms' length, and then I looked up and saw that Adrian had just come in. He was looking at me, and from his expression I just knew that some time during the party he was bound to come looking for me to repeat everything he had said before.' She paused before going on, her feelings at that time very real to her, then said, 'On reflection I can see I must have seemed cruel, but I'd honestly thought I'd tried everything else. So when Vance started to become amorous, and with Adrian looking on, instead of slapping Vance down, I let him get on with it.'

'Thinking to show Adrian that if you were the only one for him, then he wasn't the only one for you,' said Thorp, his face still serious.

'Something like that,' she agreed, not feeling very good about it now.

'You had no idea the man you were dancing with

intended to follow you upstairs?'

'None at all. I'd had enough of the party by then, and for all I'd told Adrian I was on my way to the bathroom, I went upstairs to collect my cloak. I didn't know in which bedroom Primrose had put it, and had just discovered it wasn't in the bedroom used for that purpose at her last party, when before I knew what was happening Vance was there behind me, pushing me inside and putting out the light. I suppose since I hadn't repulsed him he felt I was agreeable, but I wasn't, and the next thing I knew was he'd got me on the bed and I was discovering he'd already parted with his shirt. Then the light went on and you stood there. I came out of that room before Vance had a chance to realise that it wasn't his night.'

'And shortly after that you and Sophie left the party.'

To tell him Sophie hadn't been with her would mean giving Sophie away, so she settled for a brief, 'Yes.'

'And where does Davy come into this? Was he at the party? Did he follow you home?'

'No,' said Jancis, and went on to explain while Thorp listened with seemingly every patience, of the way the four of them, herself. William, Sophie and Davy, had all gone around together when they had all lived at Little Bramington. How Davy had a standing invitation to a bed much in the same way as Sophie had. 'My brother William had gone off to Greece to work on a dig only that morning,' she explained. 'I hadn't seen Davy in over twelve months, but when I got home there he was asleep on my doorstep. He was going off to Paris in the morning with some friends,' she added, 'and only wanted a bed for the night.'

She sensed Thorp was believing her, and, much happier telling the truth than lying to him all the time, she sought for a truth that wouldn't involve letting him know Sophie hadn't come home all night.

'Since Sophie's things were already in William's room,

I decided to bunk in with her,' she told him, ending, 'When Davy thanked me for the use of my bed the next morning, that was all, in his quaint way, that he was thanking me for.'

There followed a silence that seemed to stretch endlessly. But having anticipated the full and extreme pleasure she would experience when Thorp knew exactly how mistaken he had been about her, Jancis found that pleasure sadly lacking when at last he spoke.

'If you'd like to take a swing at me now, Jancis, I promise I won't stop you. I jumped in with both feet, didn't I?'

'You believe me?'

'Were you lying?'

'No,' she said. 'No.'

She stood up then, prepared to go—and had no idea, until she had taken a step towards the door and found Thorp's hand on her shoulder restraining her, that when she had said she hadn't been lying, he had taken her to mean she had been lying about the *whole* of what she had told him since he had entered the study, and not just the part she had only now revealed.

'It seems to me that I've treated you very badly,' he said over her shoulder. Then what he said next after a brief pause, had her body going rigid. 'I think the only decent thing I can do is to marry you.'

'Marry me!' she exclaimed aghast, not pretending that the idea of marrying him was enough to give her screaming nightmares. 'Good grief,' she exclaimed, spinning round, 'you don't have to marry me just because you'd got me pegged as a tramp and now find out I'm not!' She was so completely stunned, she forgot entirely the first half of their conversation.

Thorp's eyes took on a warm look she thought must be from anger because there was nothing funny in this situation, and anyway, he didn't know how to laugh.

'Surely you haven't forgotten what we did last night?' he asked, watching as the colour flooded her face as she remembered what she had told him. 'I'm not having any child of mine born illegitimate,' he told her sternly.

'I—er—I m-may not be pregnant,' she said. Impossible to back down now and say he hadn't touched her if she didn't want to be made to look a lying fool.

'But from what you've told me you well could be,' he put in. 'From what you've told me of your lack of experience in that field it goes without saying you weren't prepared not to conceive.'

'Well—er—we'll have to wait and see,' she said, which, she thought, left it nicely in the air.

'No, Jancis, I don't think so.' His mind was already made up, by the look of it. 'I feel badly enough as it is that I unknowingly took your innocence last night. It will grieve me for evermore that I may have been more rough with you in my—drunken state than I would otherwise have been. And I certainly don't intend you should have the worry of not having my support should you or should you not be pregnant as a result. No,' he said, and she could tell there was no arguing with him, 'we'll be married without delay.'

'I don't want to . . .' 'marry you', she had started to say, but her voice fizzled out as one look at him was all that was needed to have the conviction growing that he would keep her there all day until she agreed. She was growing confused, she thought, her eyes leaving his to take in his stubborn chin. Thorp Kingman wasn't a man who gave in easily, and more than anything at that moment she needed to be alone.

'I'll marry you,' she heard herself say, and tacked hastily on the end, 'But not straight away. I . . . I need time to think.'

She did, but not time to think about marrying him. What she needed was time to think how she was going to get out of this mess. She couldn't say she hadn't brought it on herself. She had thought she was being so clever too. But Sophie had warned her, her warning ignored, that just when you thought you were the one to have Thorp scuttled, then you found you were the one who was dangling over a barrel.

'We'll need to talk some more,' he agreed, when she hadn't thought he would. Jancis felt pale, wondered if she looked as pale as she felt, but didn't think he had taken that into account when he agreed to let her go. 'I'd better be getting back to the lab now anyway,' he said. 'If I know my niece she's taking every advantage of my absence to make a thorough nuisance of herself with Gareth.'

Relief spreading through her that she was at last able to get away from him, Jancis moved to the door. She found Thorp there before her, pausing before he turned the handle.

'Don't worry about a thing,' he instructed. 'Just remember that you are now engaged to me, and that I'll look after you.'

He then opened the door and she shot through it as though scalded. She thought she heard the sound of a laugh behind her as she hurried up the stairs to her room, but knew it was just her overwrought nerves that had imagined that. Thorp Kingman didn't know how to laugh. And besides, he couldn't know that the very idea of being engaged to him was enough to blow her mind.

Fifteen minutes later she was still in her room, hardly crediting that Thorp Kingman had actually asked her to marry him, and even more difficult to credit, that she had actually *agreed*!

She wouldn't marry him, of course. Marriage to him was out of the question. Why, she didn't even like the man, did she? Of course she didn't, she told herself, wondering why the heck she had even to think about it. Thorp might be able to stir some wayward streak in her when he kissed her, but that was just a quirk in her she had never before encountered. Not that he would have another chance to kiss her—even if believing they were engaged he now thought himself entitled.

Slowly she allowed the whole scene in the study to replay itself in her mind. And as one emotion after another went through her, gradually from a complete sense of unreality, bit by bit, her world began to right itself and she began to see this as a heavensent opportunity of evening up every insult she had received from Mr Thorp Kingman. Sophie's notion that Thorp always had the last laugh just had to crumble if she went through with being engaged to him. He obviously had no doubts that there was a possibility of his having made her pregnant. Well, tough luck on him. He couldn't want to marry her any more than she wanted to marry him, but she'd string him along for a few weeks. Make him bitterly regret getting drunk last night. Make him sweat it out as long as she could before she told him she wasn't pregnant after all and that he had no need, for the possible sake of her unborn child, to bury his dislike of her and marry her.

She was still in her room when Sophie came looking for her. What the expression on her face was she didn't know, but it certainly stopped Sophie in mid-flight as she barged straight in.

'Gareth Logan said——' she began, and stopped. 'I say, you look like a cat who's just inherited a whole creamery. What gives?'

Hastily Jancis altered her expression. 'Was I looking like that?' she asked aiming for some of Sophie's innocence when she'd been up to something. Then heading her off. 'Did you see Gareth?'

Neatly Sophie took the bait, her expression becoming dreamy. 'Oh, Jancy,' she sighed, 'I've never felt this way about a man before! Gareth's . . .'

Jancis listened to Sophie rapturising over Gareth
Logan, having suffered the pangs of love herself feeling a
deep empathy with her dear scatterbrained friend. Sophie
had been singing Gareth's praises, seeking her advice
about love, for all of ten minutes when like a bolt from
the blue Jancis realised she felt no pain in talking about
love. It no longer hurt to think of Shaw Pengelly. I'm
over him! she thought with a sense of wonder. It didn't
hurt!

Barely had she come round from that shattering dis-
covery when Sophie, gradually becoming aware that she
had no need to emphasise what being in love felt like,
because Jancis seemed to know, said gently:

'You know about love too, don't you?' Then, shedding
her dream world for a moment as her lively brain searched
further, 'Who is he? Can you tell me, Jancy?'

Sophie paused as she saw a shutter come down over her
face, and having no idea that the last thing Jancis was
going to tell her was that the feeling she was feeling now,
her hopes and dreams of what might be, could turn into
rancid, agonising despair if that love wasn't mutual, her
mind did a rapid file check on the men they both knew,
and then she gasped:

'Crikey,' and her eyes growing wide, 'is it Thorp?'

'Thorp!' Jancis exclaimed startled. Lord above, when
Sophie's imagination went to work, it knew no bounds.

'Is it, Jancy?' Sophie pressed, unable to read her expression, but mistaking the scoffing laugh Jancis emitted
for a laughing attempt to head her off the right track, 'It
is, isn't it?' she said, her conclusions tying up nicely with
the thought that no two people could be so antagonistic
to each other on the surface and yet so often shut themselves away in the study where they could be alone together.

Jancis delayed too long in answering, her mind having
a field day thinking that with Sophie having got the bit

between her teeth she would have to reveal everything that had taken place between her and Thorp. Then she recalled, as she had when she had rushed from her room last night, that with Sophie thinking so much of her uncle to tell her how vile he had been just wasn't on.

'Does he feel the same way?' Sophie asked excitedly, and Jancis could see that already she was tickled pink at the idea.

'No. No, he doesn't,' she said firmly, hardly realising that in hastily denying that Thorp was in love with her, she had forgotten to deny that she herself was in love with him.

'Oh, Jancy,' whispered Sophie sympathetically, and before Jancis could tell her her sympathy was wasted, Sophie's grey matter was again going into action. 'How do you know he doesn't love you?'

'Of course he doesn't love me,' Jancis replied, having no doubt that if Thorp Kingman felt anything at all for her it was more likely to be a feeling of hate than love. That thought irritated her, and she opened her mouth to rapidly close this conversation when Sophie said:

'You can't know that for sure. I mean, no man makes a point of getting a girl alone purely to tell her he doesn't love her.' She thought some more. 'Well,' she qualified, 'only if she'd been making a thorough nuisance of herself. And since the sparks invariably fly when the two of you are in the same room, albeit under the cover of politeness, it can't be said that he's seen you drooling over him.'

'Drooling over him!' Jancis ejaculated. 'Honestly, Sophie, you're the . . .'

'What did he want to see you in the study for?' Sophie wanted to know. But Jancis had had enough.

'It was a private matter.' she said severely.

'Ho, ho,' said Sophie, refusing to be repressed. Then slyly, catching Jancis unawares, 'Er—did he kiss you?'

Her nose in the air, Jancis answered tightly, 'No, he

didn't,' and had no clue why she should slip up and add, almost to herself, but not as quietly as she thought, 'Not this morning he didn't.'

It was too late to retract it. Sophie had heard, and as scarlet colour flooded Jancis' face, a knowing look crossed Sophie's expression, but wisely she bit her tongue on the almost irrepressible urge to find out more.

'Will you promise not to slap me if I promise not to call you Auntie?' she dared.

'Sophie,' said Jancis sharply, 'shut up!' But she had to turn away to grin. It was impossible to stay mad at Sophie for long.

Suspecting when she vetoed her suggestion of a walk that Sophie wanted to stay in the vicinity of the house where she stood more chance of catching a glimpse of Gareth, Jancis didn't press her. Fortunately she hadn't mentioned Thorp again, though Gareth Logan's name frequently came up that day.

Jancis too had much on her mind. Happy to be over Shaw, she experienced the temptation in a weak moment to confess to Thorp the truth that nothing had happened in that bed last night. Then she thought of the way he had been ready to believe the very worst of her and the temptation was overcome. Let him stew, she thought. Let him think he had despoiled her. Let him think for his sins that he was going to marry her. He deserved a few sleepless nights.

Savouring the joy to be extracted from deceiving him, she tried to concentrate on what Sophie was telling her about Gareth Logan. So far she had learned that he was twenty-six, seemingly as dedicated to his work as Thorp and admired the Professor tremendously.

'Professor!' Jancis forgot she had decided not to discuss Thorp to exclaim.

'Everybody has some skeleton in their cupboard,' Sophie chuckled as they crossed the hall to take afternoon tea. Then her face fell into unaccustomed solemn lines as the door opened and a tall, thinnish man came in.

He had a mop of dark chestnutty hair, and from the white overall he was wearing Jancis gathered this must be Gareth Logan. She was sure he would merely have nodded as he passed, but after a moment when Sophie seemed for one of the rare times to be struck dumb, she found her voice and halted him to introduce him to Jancis.

'We're just about to have tea,' she said quickly after he had briefly shaken the hand Jancis had extended and taken a step away from them. 'Can you spare a minute to join us? It's . . .'

'Thorp's waiting for some notes,' Gareth answered.

'Perhaps you can come back when you've delivered them,' Sophie suggested hopefully.

'We're busy just now,' he excused himself, and disappeared into the study.

'What's the betting he's mopping his brow at such a close shave?' said Sophie, not seeming to be put out that the offer of taking tea with two far from plain young ladies should be rejected. Then, seriously, 'Do you know, Jancy, I reckon I've got an uphill job in front of me there.'

Ready to go down to dinner that night and hoping that Thorp would be going out, Jancis surveyed her reflection in the mirror and thought if her 'fiancé' had no plans to go out then there was nothing about her appearance that should put him off his food. She had dressed with care, selecting a plum-coloured velvet dinner gown, its rounded neck showing off the perfection of her creamy skin, its long sleeves giving the dress a touch of elegance. Her hair she had done up in a most becoming knot, adding to the elegance, leaving her nape bare, her neck regal and inviting.

Why she should be feeling nervous she couldn't think, because she held all the high cards. The game was hers. Perhaps the niggling remembrance that Sophie thought

Thorp was a master at trumping a trick one thought was theirs might have something to do with it. But what trump he could hold she couldn't possibly think, since he had no recollection of what had happened after his head had hit her pillow last night. While she—she had been coldly awake to the fact that not one single solitary thing had happened.

All the same, she had no intention of being parted from Sophie tonight—that was if Thorp did intend to dine at home. And since he had said they would talk again on the subject of their marriage, should he issue yet another command that he would like to see her in his study, then she had every intention of being stricken with the severest of headaches.

'Golly!' said Sophie, coming into her room in her usual spirited way and seeing Jancis bedecked in her gorgeous dinner gown.

Jancis couldn't meet her eyes, and wished she had decided to wear any of the other dresses she had brought with her. Sophie herself was dressed in a pretty though not her best dinner dress, and she realised then that from Sophie's angle it would look as though she had done herself up to make a killing.

'I can't wait to see Thorp's face,' Sophie said. 'Come on, he'll be expecting us to join him in the drawing room.'

'He's dining at home, then?' Jancis questioned, as though it was a matter of complete unconcern to her, which gained her nothing from Sophie but a look that said she didn't think the plum velvet would have had an airing had it been just they two.

It was something of a let-down to have reminded herself yet again before they went into the drawing room that she was the one who was going to gain the most satisfaction from this charade, and then to find that the drawing room was empty. She relaxed, declining Sophie's offer of a drink, and decided Thorp must have gone out—then turned to find he had come into the room and was silently watching her. Her relaxed feeling fled. Whether he admired what he saw, she couldn't tell, but it was a moment or two before he moved, then he came over to her.

'You look perfectly charming, Jancis,' he said softly, and she still wasn't sure if he meant it or if he was just saying that because he thought it was expected of him now that he thought they were engaged.

Unable to remember the last time she had felt so lacking in confidence, she was amazed to find she was actually trembling as she muttered a quiet, 'Thank you.'

She doubted Thorp had heard her, because he had moved over to the drinks tray where Sophie was helping herself from the sherry decanter and was asking her what mischief she had been up to that day.

'I've been as good as gold,' Sophie replied, her eyes wide and innocent, though regretful at having missed what reaction if any Thorp had shown to her friend's beauty. 'I think I've turned over a new leaf, Thorp.'

'If only I could believe that,' he teased, one corner of his mouth turning up, not unpleasantly, Jancis, who had been watching, found herself thinking.

Hurriedly she turned away, not wanting to like anything about him, and concentrated her attention on a small painting by a well known Dutch artist on the wall.

'And have you been as good as gold too, Jancis?' Thorp enquired, taking a sip from the glass in his hand.

'Left to my own devices, I always am,' she muttered, and turned away, wanting to grin at the sauce of her remark and not wanting him to see it.

Sophie asking what time off Gareth Logan had cut across any rejoinder he would have made. And though he had previously told his niece to leave his assistant alone, Thorp told her that Gareth officially worked Monday to

Friday nine to five, though, with that corner of his mouth turning up again, he added that sometimes they got carried away with whatever they were doing and often worked well past five.

'So I expect Gareth has some time off due to him for all the overtime he puts in,' Sophie said thoughtfully, and obviously too from the way Thorp laughed.

His laugh disturbed her as much as his lopsided grin had done. She didn't want him to change, didn't want to see this warmer side to him. She wanted him to remain as horrible as she knew he was.

'Smitten chicken?' she heard him ask Sophie seriously.

'You could say that,' was the reply.

Over dinner Thorp kept the conversation light. And in contrast to the way last night he had addressed very few remarks to her, tonight he made a point of not leaving Jancis to sit quietly with her own thoughts.

There was a sticky moment when a lull in the conversation had Sophie remembering she had left her downstairs last night watching television, and she asked if the programme had been worth watching, adding:

'At any rate you'll be able to tell William who did it.' She then turned to her uncle to explain, 'William is Jancy's brother.'

'I know,' said Thorp.

'You know?' Sophie questioned thoughtfully.

'Jancis told me about him.'

'Oh,' said Sophie, looking from one to the other, a world of speculation in her look as she wondered what else the two had discussed. Then, edging her way slowly, 'The four of us used to have some terrific times together.'

Knowing Sophie was itching to find out if Thorp knew about Davy, Jancis gave her a look that said so much for her promise to keep quiet about him, which checked her from adding anything else. Though since Thorp had intercepted the look, it wasn't lost on him.

GALLANT ANTAGONIST   111

'You mean, you, Jancis, William and Davy?' he enquired smoothly, effectively releasing Sophie from her promise since he obviously knew all about Davy.

'You've told Thorp,' she said, turning to Jancis. Then, merrily, 'I thought it a bit daft of you not to let me tell him it was our love-brother Davy who'd spent the night at your place when I wanted to.' Then, forgetting herself, she said wistfully, 'I wish I had seen him, but . . .' Realising she had made a slip, she looked quickly at Thorp to find he was looking at her, his expression telling her she wasn't going to be able to leave it there.

'Interesting,' he observed. 'Am I going to learn, Sophie, how Jancis came to see Davy, yet you, who if my information is correct, spent the night in the same flat, didn't?'

Believing Sophie to be mentally putting her powers of invention to full use, Jancis was surprised to hear her say impishly, 'It's a fair cop, guv.'

But when she told him how she had got her to drive her car back to the flat, and Thorp had received the answer to his question that Jancis had never driven a sports car before, she discovered he was very far from amused. And it wasn't that he was angry because she had hoodwinked him that night, but because of the risk she had allowed Jancis to run.

With astonishment, Jancis heard him read Sophie the Riot Act, telling her that the sole purpose in her father changing her car insurance to owner driver only was to prevent her from loaning it out; to ensure that she allowed no one else to drive her car.

There wasn't a smile to be seen on Sophie's sweet face as Thorp told her her father's trust in her intelligence had been grossly misplaced, and he was bitingly angry when he ended:

' . . . and had Jancis had an accident, which could well have happened driving a car new to her and in the lunatic fashion she drove away from the party, besides the permanent damage she might have done herself, there would have been no insurance cover for injury inflicted to her or any other person involved. Can you imagine the colossal damages your father would have to pay had that happened?'

'I'm sorry, Thorp,' Sophie whispered.

'I should damn well think you are,' he said heavily. 'It's just as well while I have charge of you that that vehicle is staying in London.'

'Yes, Thorp,' said Sophie meekly, and to Jancis's horror asked if she might go to her room.

'I think to date that's the best idea you've had,' he said, turning his attention away from her brimming eyes and focussing his gaze on Jancis, who had half risen to go with her. 'There's no need for you to go and hold her hand.'

The sheer authority in his voice caused her to be seated again, and as the door closed behind Sophie, he added, 'I've no doubt that young lady will have dried her tears before she's reached the top of the stairs and she'll be hatching something new.' So he didn't believe in Sophie's tears, and she wouldn't go hungry because they had finished their meal and had been drinking coffee. 'Besides which, you and I have a few things of our own we have to discuss, wouldn't you agree?'

Jancis didn't. She had seen Thorp in several moods tonight. She had seen him laugh, and been fascinated by the sound as much as seeing the difference in his face his strong white teeth in evidence, his look lightened. She had seen him play the stern guardian for all Sophie was of an age when a guardian should not be required, but definitely was where the Sophies of this world were concerned. And between these two sides, not counting the charm he had shown in including her into the mealtime conversation, she knew herself confused. And she knew then it was going to take everything she possessed not to have her blurting out the real truth since she was sure the discussion they were to have was about Thorp's intention to marry her. But she mustn't tell him. She had witnessed his anger with Sophie, and the fight in her felt floored at just the thought of having that sort of anger directed at her.

CHAPTER EIGHT

AT Thorp's suggestion they left the dining room and were in the drawing room before Jancis' wits had returned, and she remembered she had planned to have a headache if this very eventuality looked like happening. Too late now. He was too sharp not to see through that excuse. Her chin tilted stubbornly as her backbone stiffened. She wasn't afraid of him. She wasn't running away at the first hurdle. She owed him and then some.

'Would you like a drink?' he offered, his manner easy, not at all agressive or hard as she had expected it would be—particularly since he must be cursing like hell the fact that according to his code of ethics he was now going to have to pay for his folly of last night.

'No, thank you,' she answered politely, thinking she would need to keep a clear head if her intention to lead him up the garden path was to be successful.

'In that case why don't we sit down?' he suggested, indicating the settee and ignoring the drinks table, which caused her to think that he too was determined to keep a very clear head this evening.

Deciding against the settee, she promptly selected one of the well upholstered chairs in the room. She saw him suck in his cheeks as though to hide amusement, and her warring instincts against him took on fresh fuel from knowing he was fully aware she was nervous of him sitting next to her, lest he should consider he now had a right to sample some of what he couldn't remember from last night.

Taking the chair across from her, Thorp didn't immediately bring the talk, as she had expected, straight to their engagement. Instead, he sat back with his eyes going over her, missing nothing of her tiny waistline or her well formed bust; his gaze resting on her face and finally going to the elegance of her silky titian hair.

'You were beautiful as a child, Jancis,' he observed, his manner casual. 'It hardly seems possible that the woman is even more beautiful.'

His remark about her beauty was unexpected. But even more unexpected was the fact that he had remembered that incident of eleven years ago.

'I didn't—think you would have remembered me,' she said slowly, feeling ridiculously inadequate. Probably because she had prepared herself for a very different conversation, she told herself, struggling to stay on top.

'I've never seen such hate in a child's eyes,' he answered. 'I hurt more than your rear end then, didn't I?'

Useless trying to look as though she couldn't recall her feelings at that time. By saying she didn't think he would remember her, she had revealed that she too had never forgotten.

'I hated you,' she admitted. 'I was twelve years old, with part of me trying to pretend I was a young lady.'

'And I put you right back among the infants,' Thorp remarked. 'In my defence, I didn't think I had walloped you that hard.' It had felt like it at the time, but perhaps he had tempered that spanking to her size. 'Though since I'd only taken delivery of that car the day before, I probably thought I had a right to be angry.' He broke off to give her a level look, then asked quietly, 'Still hate me, Jancis?'

'It isn't important, is it,' she said, her chin at a haughty angle, 'whether I hate you or not?'

'I think it is,' he replied, his voice still quiet. 'I think since we're soon to be married you should give me some idea of how you regard me.'

Soon to be married! With an effort she kept her face straight. This was what she wanted, wasn't it—to lead him on to think she had fallen in with his ridiculous assertion that it was the only way open to them.

'Surely how I regard you isn't important,' she said, thinking if she told him how she really felt about him he would cancel out all thoughts of marriage too.

He turned his head to one side, considering her levelly. 'Perhaps you're right,' he said after a moment. 'You've admitted I didn't have to rape you last night to slake my desire. So in one aspect at least our marriage shouldn't run into problems.'

Colour flared into her face. 'Th-there's more to marriage than just sex,' she told him snootily, knowing very little about either.

'I agree,' said Thorp, and knocked her neatly off her lofty perch by adding, 'But since, without effort apparently, for I could hardly have been my normal self when I took you, there must be something about my lovemaking that turns you on, we know we won't have any trouble in that department. You were a virgin before my visit to your room, I believe you told me?'

Jancis remained quiet, distinctly not liking the turn this conversation was taking. She had thought, knowing he would want to talk about his offer to marry her some time, that that talk would be purely of the formalities, the arrangements to be made.

'Was it true?' he insisted, and Jancis dropped her eyes at his being determined to know if he had been her first lover; clearly he still had doubts about it.

'I didn't lie,' she said, raising her eyes quickly to catch him frowning at her answer. She knew what he was thinking and it infuriated her that of all the lies she had told him, he should refuse to believe one of the few truths. 'I'd never been to bed with anyone before I slept with you,' she snapped angrily.

'Is that a fact?' he said slowly, giving her a hard look. 'You must be—twenty-three now. You have everything in the right place plus a beautiful face. Are you expecting me to believe that no man has ever tried to get you into bed?'

'Just because it's been tried it doesn't mean I've been tempted,' she said shortly, conscious she was losing her temper and knowing she was far from being the cool person she wanted to be when dealing with him.

'You don't strike me as a frigid woman,' he said, his eyes holding hers steadily. 'I've seen the sparks flying from your eyes, felt the sting of your hand when passion is about you. And aside from last night, when I was able to arouse you without too much trouble, it seems, are you now seriously trying to tell me you've never before felt tempted?'

Where before her cheeks had been a warm pink, now they were white. 'I . . .' she gasped, memories crowding her. She no longer loved Shaw, but pain was there again, pain this time of hurt pride. Had she been willing Shaw would have made love to her and then gone on his way without a second's thought.

'What is it?' Unbeknown to her Thorp had witnessed her hurt and had come to sit on the arm of her chair. He tipped up her face. 'Did I strike a painful chord?' he asked.

'Yes, damn you!' she fired, her eyes clashing with his, feeling better suddenly, and angry with it. 'And yes—yes, I was tempted—once.'

'And did you go over the edge?' he asked mercilessly.

'No, I didn't. I told you I hadn't.'

Her temper soaring that this wasn't the way the scene was supposed to go, she wanted only to go to her room. She had told him something she had never told another soul and she didn't know who she was more angry with, him or herself. Yet she didn't seem able to stop.

'I was in love with him,' she said recklessly, pulling her face from his hand and jumping to her feet. 'But . . .' She had said too much, and didn't want to tell him any more.

Aware that she had revealed secret parts of herself, she made a rush for the door. But Thorp had her by the arms before she reached it.

'Don't dash off just when the conversation is getting interesting,' he said, cool in relation to her heat, and turned her so she was facing him, his hands ensuring that she couldn't get away. 'Are you still in love with him?' His voice was sharp, unexpected when he had been so cool, and caused the answer to fire from her.

'No,' she said tautly, then, more slowly, 'I thought I was. I was—definitely,' she amended, remembering those months of pain. She smiled a mirthless smile. 'He said he loved me too. But had I given in to him all I would have been would be another star in his little black book.'

Thorp had no trouble in following her, and for a second she wondered if he too had an asterisk system, before the thought died. Thorp was too mature for that sort of adolescent behaviour. A frown wrinkled her brow at that. It was as though she thought him a much finer person than Shaw. Really she must get to her room, her thinking was all haywire.

'Let me go, Thorp,' she said, her voice growing husky.

'Is it possible you weren't in love with him at all?' he suggested, ignoring her request.

'I was in love with him,' she argued, her voice growing stronger that he should attempt to minimise all the pain that loving had caused.

'Yet being a full-blooded, passionate woman you couldn't allow the man you loved to make love to you?'

There was scepticism there. Clearly he was doubting she had loved Shaw if she hadn't been able to let him make love to her yet had allowed him to do so without a fight, there being no bruise or scratch on either of them that morning to evidence that she had clawed and fought before giving in.

'Well, I don't love him now,' she said flatly.

'Which is just as well in the circumstances,' he replied, 'since you've already agreed to marry me.'

Was she supposed to gather from that that had she still been in love with Shaw then Thorp's offer of marriage would be cancelled? I'm getting more and more confused by the minute, she thought, and then needed all her wits about her, for he said:

'And that brings us, I think, to the reason why I asked you to join me in this room.'

Her face expressed a query, though really she was playing for time, considering now that she just wasn't up to playing him along; perhaps tomorrow . . .

'We have to set a date for our wedding,' he reminded her in answer to her enquiring look.

'There's no hurry to do that, is there?' she said, pretending to stifle a yawn. 'I really am very tired.'

Thorp didn't comment on the fact that he had spent an exacting day working in his laboratory while she had done nothing beyond lazing around reading magazines and playing Canasta with Sophie. But instead he said rather sharply:

'I think there's every need. Have you forgotten you could well be pregnant?'

Hoist with her own petard, Janeis grew irritated. She found him the most maddening, frustrating of men. 'Oh— Oh, don't be stuffy!' she threw at him, and felt alarm begin to grow when the grip he had on her arms tightened and she saw the narrowing of his eyes. He didn't take kindly to being called stuffy, she couldn't doubt that.

'You called me something similar once before,' he grated rather than said. And while her frowning alarm threatened to consume her, he hauled her close up to his hard body. 'You lived to regret it then, I believe,' he added, and before she could stop him his mouth had taken possession of hers.

She struggled to be free, but all to no avail. Thorp

wasn't finished with kissing her yet and wasn't ready to heed any protest she made.

'Stop it!' she breathed when his lips left hers to wander in tantalising light kisses on her throat and chest.

For answer his hands, now at the back of her, pressed her closer to him. She didn't want him to kiss her, she didn't, she kept repeating to herself, renewing her struggles to break away whenever she had the chance.

Then his mouth was covering hers again, his tongue coming out to moisten the stubborn line of her tightly closed lips, and a thrill of pure pleasure awakened itself in the lower half of her, and without her volition her lips parted to emit a low groan as she experienced a need for him that should have been alien to her, but over which she had no control.

'Relax,' he whispered softly, 'I'm not going to hurt you.'

His voice, gentle, persuasive, was unlike any tone she had heard from him before, and her hands that had been pushing at his arms trying for release were suddenly useless and all she could do, as his mouth claimed her now parted lips, was to hold on to him.

This time when Thorp kissed her there was no thought of hanging back. He was evoking feelings inside her that even Shaw hadn't been able to arouse. Though Shaw had no part in her thoughts just then, her whole being belonged to Thorp and she wanted more—much more than kisses. She wanted to caress him, but where shyness was holding her back, she had no idea why he was holding back. His kisses, over her throat, to her ears, to where the neck of her dress allowed him, were driving her mad, but his hands were firm on her back as though cemented there, and she could hardly think that they were so because he felt to let them rove would mean there would be no holding back because he had her so that she knew no such restraint.

Thorp brought his head back and looked into her eyes. What he saw there she could only guess at, but his eyes were no longer the ice-cold grey she remembered. The ice had melted and she just knew that he was on fire for her, the way she was on fire for him.

She wanted to ask him to kiss her again, but the words wouldn't come. But heedless that she wasn't thinking straight, heedless that this had never been part of her plan, she just had to have him kiss her once more. And it was Jancis who did the kissing the next time, not realising until much later that this was the point where Thorp was in fact silently saying, 'I think that's enough—any more and I won't be responsible.'

Her hands tightened on his shoulders and when his head did not come down to meet her, she raised herself on tiptoe and pressed her parted lips against his. A groan came from him that sounded very much like the one that had escaped her. Then his hands gripped her once, and then she knew she had been playing with fire. But that didn't matter, because that was what she wanted too.

Or so she thought, until Thorp picked her up and carried her to the settee. She was still thinking so, still riding on the high voltage of feeling he had aroused in her, when he slid the zip of her dress down. The air felt cold on her skin, she felt Thorp move her dress from her shoulders, and it was at that point that alarm began to jostle with excitement.

Without requesting her permission he exposed her full breasts to his gaze, and it was only then, shyness at having a man see her semi-nudity for the first time mingling with a definite feeling of alarm, that the excitement of wanting Thorp to possess her dimmed.

'Oh God!' she heard him breathe, just as though he was having some private struggle as he gazed at her swollen curves. If there was some conflict within him it was lost as with a jerky movement his hands gripped her waist and then his head came down and his mouth began a lingering sortie on the deep rose tip of her breast.

Excitement flooded through her again, and this time it was she who found herself in conflict—a conflict of emotions. Excitement tried to oust alarm. Thorp's hands came to caress her breasts, a gentle, sensitive touch that had her fighting to get common sense to join on the side of alarm and banish that excitement that had her moaning with pleasure. For a split second common sense was on top, and in a now-or-never move she took advantage of that split second to push his hands away, another half a breath and she would be lost.

Panicking madly in case he was too aroused to let her go, she shot off the settee, her dress anyhow about her, only to find he was right behind her, his hands on her bare arms staying her.

'Don't you think,' he said, his voice sounding thick and unlike his in her ears, 'that you've left it a little too late to tell me you're "not a girl like that"?'

'It's your fault that I no longer am,' she found from somewhere, not recognising her own voice either, choked as it was with emotion.

'As you say,' Thorp replied, and she was sure, though she wasn't turning around to find out, that a careless shrug accompanied that remark.

Wanting only to be gone, her fingers trembling as she agitatedly straightened her bra, she felt a regretful sort of relief wash over her as she felt his hands at her back zipping up her dress. She had taken hasty footsteps towards the door when his voice next reached her.

'Shall I come to your room again tonight?' he asked, but if he was waiting for a reply there was no one there to answer him.

Wondering if a couple of aspirins would sedate her, Jancis felt her mind was still a tangled mass of crossed wires much, much later. She had no recollection of getting undressed and into bed or jamming a chair under the handle of the door. She presumed she had rinsed her face and cleaned her teeth, her night-time habit, but she had no recollection of that either.

What in God's name had got into her downstairs? She didn't even like the man! Another groan escaped her and she pushed agitated fingers through hair that only now she realised was not in the classic knot she had dressed it in. Vaguely she recalled Thorp removing the confining pins while at the same time kissing her so fiercely. Oh, lord! she groaned again. She didn't want to think about it. But not wanting to think and fighting with all the will at her command couldn't stop those remembered moments from storming in. Nothing would oust the remembrance of the way Thorp Kingman, seemingly without effort, had made her like putty in his hands.

Her travelling alarm showed half past four before she slipped out of bed and removed the chair from the door. She didn't want Carol broadcasting it all round the village that when she had brought the morning tea one of the guests at the Manor had barricaded herself in. Her tormented thoughts gradually gave way to exhaustion, and at last she fell asleep with her decision made. As soon as possible tomorrow morning she was going to pack her bags and get out of here. For the first time in her life she was running away. But—but she'd had it.

Her plans to leave Widefields Manor with all possible haste took a tremendous setback before she had barely opened her eyes. A sound in the room must have disturbed her, for she came awake to see from her travelling clock that it had gone ten.

Ten past ten? she thought, astonished, then the remembrance of what had happened last night zoomed powerfully in. The unbelievability of her own wayward emotions hit her, and then she became aware that she had company.

'Thank God you're awake at last,' said a beaming Sophie, coming to plonk herself down on the bed. 'I've been in to see you half a dozen times, but you've been dead to the world.'

'I . . .' Jancis began, coming to life and thinking that since Sophie was here she might as well tell her now that she was leaving and get it over with. But Sophie wasn't giving her time to say anything.

'I thought if I left you alone with Thorp something might develop,' she crowed happily. 'But goodness, Jan, I never expected things to move so fast!'

'So fast?' Jancis repeated stupidly, thinking, Oh, lord, what's gone on now?

'And you told me you didn't believe in love at first sight,' Sophie prattled on, as dread at what was coming next entered Jancis's being. 'Thorp isn't one to show much emotion, but he too looked as though he had a share in your creamery when he told me you and he were engaged.'

Jancis closed her eyes, feeling faint. She kept her eyes closed as surging anger gave faintness a hiding. She didn't doubt he had looked smug. He meant to marry her regardless of how she felt about it. He must have surmised that she was ready to bolt, and this was his way of making sure she stayed put. For she couldn't very well leave so soon after he had told Sophie they were engaged. He was also no doubt armed ready to tell Sophie of the possibility of her being pregnant should she deny the engagement, she realised with chagrin. And to tell Sophie the truth would mean Thorp knowing too since, loyal though Sophie was, she couldn't expect that loyalty to hold out against the pull of family loyalty. And who would end up looking stupid when Sophie in turn related to him the truth of that night? None other than Jancis Langfield, that's who.

'Don't go to sleep again, Jancy!' wailed Sophie. 'I've

been waiting ages as it is for you to tell me how it happened.'

Jancis opened her eyes, but no concrete plan formed. Sophie looked so happy sitting here, her effervescent spirits frothing over. It caused her to feel even further annoyed with Thorp.

'There's nothing to tell,' she said, trying to make her voice light. Thorp Kingman thought that by bringing their engagement out into the open he had her just where he wanted her. Well, was he in for a surprise! He was getting her nowhere near the altar. And she'd take jolly good care not to be left alone with him again. Not that she would ever behave the way she had done last night, she thought, her colour rising as again she wondered what had come over her.

'If blushes are anything to go by, there's a lot you're not going to tell me,' Sophie grinned.

'Well,' she said lamely, 'some things are private.'

And with that Sophie had to be satisfied, though she was in high spirits for the rest of the morning. While Jancis' spirits sank lower and lower. She was growing more and more angrily certain that Thorp had told Sophie they were engaged because he had suspected she intended to leave that day, and alternated between fury at what he had done and a strengthening desire to make him suffer which mixed badly with the growing trepidation of how was she ever going to look him in the face again after last night?

'You'd have thought in the circumstances Thorp would have left his beastly test tubes to have lunch with us today at least,' Sophie complained, when to Jancis' utmost relief Thorp hadn't put in an appearance. 'He might even have brought Gareth with him as a kind of celebration,' she tacked on, her eyes going dreamy again.

'I know he's very busy at the moment,' Jancis felt compelled to say, knowing nothing of the kind and hating to find herself actually making excuses for him.

'We could always go and see him in the laboratory, I suppose,' Sophie suggested hopefully, and when Jancis looked at her in alarm knowing wild horses wouldn't get her within ten yards of the laboratory, she added, 'He's not likely to turf you out the way he would me.'

'And while I'm talking to Thorp you could be talking to Gareth?'

'I have some great ideas, don't I?' smiled Sophie.

'He's busy,' Jancis said hurriedly. 'I can't interrupt him.' She caught Sophie looking at her oddly and knew she had picked up that the very idea of seeing him had her panicking. 'I just can't,' she said, looking down at her plate.

'Well, I'll be——' Sophie muttered, stunned, then, her tone softening, 'Who'd have thought it, Jancy? You're shy of him, aren't you?' Jancis continued to look at her plate, never having felt so uncomfortable in her life, and Sophie went on, 'Of course, you haven't seen him since you got engaged last night, have you? I expect I'd feel exactly the same.'

After that Sophie was so sweet for the rest of the afternoon that with them not venturing near the laboratory, Jancis was left feeling guilty at depriving her of seeing Gareth if it was really as she said it was and she was in love with him.

They had spent a companionable afternoon walking, not to the village this time, but across the fields to the side of the Manor, and returned home just as the light was fading. Her cheeks glowing from their energetic sprint to clear the fields before in the growing dusk one or other risked coming to grief by putting an unwary foot down a rabbit hole, Jancis was shocked into immobility to see Thorp coming along the hall.

'Hello, Thorp,' said Sophie breezily. 'We've been for a walk.' She turned to Jancis, who had found the use of her legs, though all her pink colour couldn't be put down to her mad sprint. 'See, I've brought your fiancée home without mishap.'

'Er—hello,' Jancis threw his way as he drew level, her eyes fastened on the top button of the lounge suit he wore.

'Hello yourself.'

His voice had a tender note to it which she knew was solely for Sophie's benefit, as was the arm that came about her and held her firmly as though he sensed she was about to pull away. Rigidly stiff in his hold, she felt his lips touch her cheek before he released her, then Sophie was informing him:

'We were going to come and see you at work this afternoon, only Jancy got shy. She was in quite a flutter about it, actually.'

Thanks very much, Sophie! Jancis thought, feeling Thorp's eyes fixed on her and, refusing to be cowed, brought her head up. He *was* looking at her, his grey eyes pinning her, and she just knew he was thinking her shyness had been little in evidence last night before she had sprung away from him.

'I say, Thorp,' said Sophie into the silence, noticing for the first time that he was wearing a lounge suit when he usually wore sweater and slacks for working, 'have you knocked off early because this is a special day?'

'I have to go into town,' he replied.

'Are you going for Jancy's ring?' she asked before he could add more.

'I don't . . .' Jancis began, and felt herself fixed with a look that said if she was going to say 'I don't want a ring' then she had better not say it. The rest of her words died in her throat, and she hated him afresh that he could do that to her.

'It's none of your business what I'm going into town for,' he told Sophie, taking his eyes from Jancis and softening his words to his niece with a smile.

No sooner had his car gone down the drive than Sophie was haring out of the house. Silently fuming that if Thorp had gone into town to buy an engagement ring then she would take great pleasure in telling him what he could do with it, Jancis stomped into the drawing room shrugging off her coat. She had calmed down a few minutes later to decide that that wasn't the purpose of his errand. He couldn't have a clue about her ring size . . . She was taken out of her thoughts by Sophie barging into the room and saying:

'Come on, put your coat on, we're going out.'

'Out?' Jancis exclaimed.

'I just caught Gareth as he was leaving. I told him you wanted something urgently from Todsbridge. He's waiting to give us a lift.'

'But I don't need anything from Todsbridge . . .' she started to protest.

'I know you don't. But it's a chance for me to be with Gareth and I thought he might think it a ruse if I said I wanted something. This way he'll think you want to buy a present for Thorp.' Sophie was already bustling her out into the hall. 'Insist on sitting in the back, there's a love.'

In no time Jancis found herself sitting in the back of Gareth Logan's sedate saloon car, drawing breath at the speed with which Sophie moved once an idea took root. Not that she could see it was doing her much good, for Gareth appeared to be the type of driver who liked to keep all his concentration on the job in hand, for all Sophie beside him was doing her best to draw him out.

His monosyllabic answers had very little effect on Sophie, however, and Jancis had to give her full marks for being a tryer. The lights of Todsbridge appeared and he turned his head to ask, 'Where would you like me to drop you?'

'Near the shopping centre,' Sophie replied for her.

Which was just as well, Jancis thought, because she hadn't got a clue to the geography of the town.

When Gareth stopped the car she thought it about time she played her part and she was out of the car like a shot. 'I'll have to dash,' she said, giving Gareth her thanks. 'The shops will be closed if I don't hurry.'

'I'll meet you at the Town Hall,' said Sophie, showing no signs of moving.

Jancis raced away, only stopping when she was sure she would be lost to Gareth's vision. A smile of resignation crossed her features. She had no idea where the Town Hall was, though since it was a cold night she hoped Sophie wouldn't keep her waiting too long.

With so many people coming from closing shops and offices, she had no difficulty in finding someone to guide her to the Town Hall. Thinking of Sophie and her mad escapades as she went, Jancis felt in a better humour than she had done all that day.

As she turned the corner of where she hoped to find the Town Hall, her good humour vanished. That was Thorp's car parked there. The number plate meant nothing to her, but those were definitely the cushions from her flat which Sophie had rested her head on last Sunday when they had journeyed from London.

With every intention of hiding in the nearest doorway should she catch sight of him, she glanced about her, registered that the tall building across the road must be the Town Hall, and then froze. For there was Thorp, and with him the woman he had obviously shed his casual clothes to keep his assignation with.

And then all hell let loose inside her.

Shock like a blow to the stomach lashed at her. He's engaged to me, she wanted to shout, no thought in her mind that the engagement wasn't to her liking. She watched, nausea grabbing at her, a sickness growing, rising as he and Aileen Forbes stopped while he said

something. They looked intimate together, so much as
though they belonged, that a blinding rage hit her that it
should be so. She hated Aileen Forbes. She felt a need to
physically attack her. Thorp didn't belong to that
sophisticated blond—he belonged to *her*!

She saw him place his hand beneath Aileen's elbow
and turn her in the direction of his car. They were coming
her way! Wings on her feet, Jancis fled round the corner.

The thought of seeing those two heads close together if
they passed in the car had her feeling sick again, and she
took to her heels and raced into an alleyway. It was dark
there, which was what she wanted. Leaning against the
wall, she shook uncontrollably before gradually the shock
of what had happened isolated itself from intuitive movement, impressions and actions.

She, who placed such a high value on fidelity, had seen
Thorp, who was supposed to be engaged to her, with
another woman. She had lost sight of the fact that she
didn't consider herself engaged to him, and saw only that
the reason for his leaving his work early was to get to
Aileen Forbes. Seeing the two of them had rocked her
where she stood, had brought to life a new screaming,
tearing emotion. A hateful, terrible, pain-racking emotion.
That emotion—jealousy. She had been violently, angrily
jealous that her fiancé, on the first day of their engagement, had hurried through his work that day so he could
change to meet another woman.

She was quite aware she was being idiotic—she didn't
have any real hold on Thorp—and yet she felt he had
broken faith with her. And she found that knowledge
shattering. Almost as shattering as knowing she didn't hate
him at all. She was in love with him.

CHAPTER NINE

It was fortunate that Sophie had been able to talk Gareth into taking her for a cup of tea while Jancis did her fictitious shopping, or she would have had a half hour wait for her. Because it took Jancis all that time before she felt she had sufficient control to move from her hideaway to the Town Hall.

Sophie sticking her head out of the car window and calling, 'Ready?' made her aware that Sophie was still with Gareth and not pedestrian as she had supposed. 'Gareth says there's not another bus back for over an hour, so he's offered to drive us back. Isn't that sweet of him?'

Gareth was his usual silent self on the return journey. 'Did you get what you wanted?' Sophie enquired of Jancis in the back, then centred all her attention on the man beside her, and didn't notice that Jancis wasn't saying a word either.

So this was why she had so eagerly accepted Thorp's lovemaking of last night, Jancis was thinking. This, then, was the reason nothing had mattered but being in his arms. She had thought herself tempted by Shaw, but it had never been that drowning feeling Thorp had aroused in her.

She saw now that she hadn't loved Shaw as fully as she had thought. That terrible and real agony she had suffered at Shaw's defection had not, she realised, been because she had loved him so overwhelmingly, but because he had shattered her faith, had broken that bond of trust she held so dearly.

And now Thorp had broken that trust too. And it hurt like hell. She tried to be logical, but logic had very little place in her emotions. It was true she hadn't considered herself engaged to Thorp, but *he* had considered them engaged. He thought, as she had led him to believe, that she might possibly be pregnant, and believing that, he had announced himself engaged to her.

But she couldn't marry him, not when on the same day he had told Sophie they were to be married she had witnessed with her own eyes his inconstancy. Dark destroying jealousy gnawed at her again when she pictured him with his lady-love, so that she was glad to find they had reached the Manor. Thanking Gareth for the lift, she left Sophie talking to him and hurried away.

Up in her room she stared at her reflection in the mirror. Her face was pale, her eyes still shocked. Never had she felt less like eating, but she would have to put a good face on it. Thorp wouldn't be in to dinner, which was a blessing, as she didn't know how she was ever going to be able to look at him again.

It amazed her that she could love him still, be so consumed with love for him yet know at the same time that he had broken faith with her. How could she love him? She selected the first dress at hand to change into while time and again as she got ready for dinner that same thought went through her mind, and with it that searing pain. Was this how her mother had felt that first time she learned that her father had been unfaithful to her?

Her love for her mother had taken an enormous jolt when she had discovered that she too had broken her marriage vows. But now, for the first time, she had some sympathy with her. Her father must have broken her heart many times over. Good luck to her, she thought, while wondering at her change of attitude. Her mother deserved some happiness from life, and in fairness she had waited until Jancis and William were of age before she had announced that she was off.

'I thought you might have worn the velvet you wore last night,' Sophie said, coming into the room and surveying the snugly fitting black dress Jancis had on. 'Though come to think of it, you look stunning in that too. I wish I was taller.'

Jancis went with her down the stairs, hoping Sophie wasn't going to ply her with questions as to where Thorp was. She just didn't feel up to defending him, and yet by the very act of loving him, he had full claim to her loyalty.

It shattered her when she went into the drawing room to find Thorp standing there looking relaxed and much at ease, wearing the same dinner jacket he had worn last night.

Startled, she made no attempt to go anywhere near him. Her mind went jealously over the time he had spent with Aileen Forbes. Had he kissed her? Had he . . .

'What can I get you, Jancis?' Thorp asked by her side, and she moved a step away when she thought his arm was going to come round her waist.

'Don't touch me!' she muttered in an angry undertone so that Sophie shouldn't hear. She couldn't bear that he should dare to think he still had a right to put his hands on her so soon after coming away from that woman.

'Not contagious, is it?' His voice, sarcastic, was equally low. Then as if noticing the woodenness of her expression, the way she looked ready to flinch if he so much as laid a finger on her, he asked sharply, 'What's wrong? What's upset you?'

'Nothing,' she said. Then she became aware that Sophie was looking at them, though supposing she would think it natural for a newly engaged couple to whisper their greetings, she forced a smile to her lips, and said more loudly, 'I won't have a drink, thank you, Thorp,' but she wouldn't have minded sneaking a bottle up to her room and drinking herself into oblivion.

Over dinner Sophie let it out that they had been into Todsbridge. 'I'd have given you a lift if you'd asked,' said Thorp, his eyes going speculatively to Jancis as though he suspected their going into town had something to do with the way she was acting.

Jancis knew she was behaving far from normally with him. She hoped Sophie would put it down to shyness if she discerned that she avoided looking into Thorp's eyes whenever he addressed a remark to her.

'Actually, Thorp,' Sophie told him candidly, 'you weren't quite the driver I wanted.'

'I see,' he said, catching on immediately. 'How long did you say you were staying?'

'Meaning you think I might disrupt Gareth if I stay here much longer?' Sophie replied. Then, her sweet face serious for once, 'It isn't a game for me this time, Thorp.'

His expression was serious as he surveyed his niece. 'Then good luck to you, poppet,' he said, raising his wine glass in her direction. His voice became teasing as he added, 'Perhaps with your schemes so fully occupied elsewhere I can hope your penchant for raising the dust wherever you go will be minimised.'

Sophie grinned, 'You could just be right!'

The excuse of a headache that Jancis had intended to use last night would come in very useful tonight, she thought, waiting her chance to put this into effect as she saw Sophie drain her coffee cup and make to leave the table.

'Would you mind if Jancis and I left you to your own devices for half an hour?' she heard Thorp address Sophie before her plea of a headache could leave her lips. She shot a disagreeable look at him, not wanting to spend five minutes alone with him, much less half an hour, but he held her look steadily. 'There are one or two matters we need to discuss.'

The way he said it sounded threatening to her, but she

remained stubbornly silent as Sophie told them generously, 'Take an hour.'

Having thought she still had a chance to use her imaginary headache as an excuse not to go with him into the drawing room, Jancis discovered that Thorp had no intention of waiting until they had left the dining room for their discussion to begin. The door had hardly clicked behind Sophie before he was saying:

'Perhaps now that we haven't a third ear, you'll tell me what's upset you?'

About to say, 'Nothing,' as she had done before, she knew suddenly that Thorp wouldn't let her get away with it. By implying that whatever was wrong was something she didn't want Sophie to hear, he knew full well that whatever had upset her it was something to do with just the two of them.

'I . . .' she began, and didn't know how to contine. To tell him the truth, that she had seen him in town with Aileen Forbes and had been torn apart by jealousy, would have him laughing so much, so long, he wouldn't be able to handle his test tubes tomorrow.

She looked across at him and saw he was waiting with every semblance of patience. From the look of him he had every intention of sitting there until midnight if need be, or however long it took for her to spit out what was troubling her, and a new kind of anger invaded her, an anger that froze all heat and left her icily angry.

'I can't marry you,' she said stonily, her chin firm, her look resolute. And for her it was for real. It had nothing to do with the fact that Thorp had no reason to marry her, but that, loving him with every part of her as she did, she just could *not* marry the kind of man she had discovered him to be.

Thorp hadn't replied to her blunt statement, but she didn't care. She didn't have feelings any more, just this terrible coldness that wouldn't leave. Her head high, she looked at him again, and the ice in her fractured marginally to see he was not looking at her with that same look that demanded answers, but was looking as though he was seeing her for the first time. He continued to stare and she wondered if he was accepting what she had said, and if now it was all right for her to go.

She moved, intending to leave with or without his permission. And then he released a long-drawn-out breath, and his voice came sounding as though he was disciplining it to stay even.

'Might I know what reason you have for breaking our engagement?' he asked steadily, and at the steadiness of his question when he knew full well that by meeting Aileen Forbes at the first oportunity that he hadn't acted like an engaged man, Jancis felt the fracture in the ice within her turned into a solid sheet once more.

'I don't know how you feel about such things as fidelity, Mr Kingman,' she said, too much arctic fury in her to want to use his first name, 'but with me it means quite a lot.'

A cold stubbornness about her, she refused to look away as his eyes narrowed at her implication that he was a cheat. His voice matched hers in coldness when he said:

'Few things come higher with me than fidelity and trust, be it business, or the subject we seem to be discussing, marriage.' He sounded so sincere she would have believed him had she not seen him in town with Aileen Forbes. And she could have hit him when he grated at her, 'You're implying that I've acted perfidiously?'

'You know damn well you have!' she flashed, her voice rising as a rapid thaw in the ice took place that he could sit there and deny it.

'There's more than one way of breaking faith,' he retorted, his tone hard. 'Obviously you saw me in town with Aileen, but instead of trusting me, you straightway rushed to put your own construction on that meeting.'

'Oh, very neat,' she snapped, angry colour coming to her cheeks. 'You sound just like my father when he used to get caught out. He could lie his way out of a paper bag too, *and* make my mother believe she was the one in the wrong to think such a thing of him.'

'Your parents are divorced, aren't they?' Thorp said calmly, when she had thought he might leap over the table and throttle her for calling him a liar. Not that she cared, but it did puzzle her that instead of either verbally or physically attacking her, he was now looking at her as though wanting to know what had made her the way she was.

'I should think the whole world knows they are,' she answered, then, cynically, 'You must have read of my father's exploits in the papers.'

Thorp didn't confirm whether he had or not, but his expression softened as he said, not ungently, 'They have scarred you, haven't they? Left you so that you can't trust an adult relationship between a man and a woman?'

She didn't want him being gentle with her. It was getting through her defences—just the way she expected her father had got through her mother's defences at the beginning. That thought was enough to have her anger icing over again.

'Not at all,' she denied woodenly, only to find her denial ignored.

'Was that what went wrong with the relationship you had with the man you were in love with?' he asked. 'Did that relationship crack because you didn't trust him enough? Because you . . .'

'No, it wasn't,' she interrupted furiously, the ice in her having boiling water poured on it. 'I told you, all he ever wanted was to get me into bed with him. He admitted the last time I saw him that while professing undying love for me he was getting what he couldn't get from me from someone else.'

Her temper fizzled out as those words shot from her, leaving her, to her horror, feeling as though she would break down and cry at any moment. Knowing her pride wouldn't stand that humiliation—how often had she seen her mother in tears after an argument with her father?— Jancis shot to her feet and would have raced through the door and up to her room had not Thorp got to the door before her.

'Let me go!' she said loudly when his arms came about her. But push him as she might, he wouldn't let her go.

'Hush,' he said softly, enfolding her to him, pressing her head against his chest. 'Hush and listen to me,' he instructed, no hardness in him at all as he gently stroked her head.

'Let me go,' she repeated, her voice not loud any more, but sounding wobbly in her own ears.

Even though she should be hating him like hell, it was heaven to be in his arms. Oh, how could she be so weak? she thought as tears spilled from her eyes. She stopped struggling to get away knowing she couldn't bear him to see her in tears. Perhaps she could discreetly dry her eyes before he let her go, though how to appear dry-eyed when that happened she didn't know, because she just didn't seem able to stop her tears from falling.

Thorp continued to hold her to him even when he must know she was no longer struggling. Then, his voice still quiet, he said, 'Had you asked me outright what I was doing meeting Aileen from her place of work, I would have told you.'

Anticipating a whole string of lies, Jancis shuddered in his arms. Don't, please don't, she wanted to say, but the words wouldn't come. 'She was expecting you to meet her?' she asked instead from her choked throat.

'I telephoned her this morning to see if she would be there,' he told her. 'She works in the planning department and is out sometimes inspecting property and from there goes straight home.'

'So you arranged a date with her?' Jancis asked in a muffled voice, the pain of the question a knife thrust to her.

'If you like,' he agreed. 'What I had to say to her I wanted to say as soon as possible, yet I didn't want to tell her over the phone.'

She stirred in his arms. Oh God, this was worse, she thought wildly. He had rushed to tell Aileen Forbes that for a joke he had got himself engaged and he wanted to tell her about it before she heard of it from someone else. She cringed; the sophisticated Aileen Forbes would be laughing herself silly! She pushed ineffectually at Thorp's chest, forgetful of her wet face, wrenching her head out of his grasp to look at him.

'Did she laugh?' she asked bitterly.

'Laugh?' Thorp echoed, as a hand came gently to the side of her face to smooth away her tears. 'No, she didn't laugh. I didn't expect that she would when I told her I wouldn't be seeing her again.'

'You told her . . .' she began, her eyes a large, misty, shimmering green. 'Oh, Thorp!' she groaned, and dived to bury her head in his chest again. There had been such sincerity in his face that she just knew he was telling her the truth. How had she ever thought of him and her father in the same thought? Thorp was nothing like him. She didn't have to look farther than his instant offer to marry her when he thought she might be pregnant. 'Oh, Thorp,' she said again, the remembrance of the way she had tricked him making her far less honourable than him, for all the whole thing had been started as a way of getting even with him.

'You believe me?' he asked quietly from somewhere above her head.

'Yes—I believe you,' she said, 'and I'm sorry . . .'

'Forget it,' he advised. 'I well remember what a sensitive child you were. I can imagine that sensitivity being battered and bruised with every confrontation you overheard between your parents. That plus the wounding you received at the hands of your ex-boy-friend have all gone to make the sort of thing you thought I was doing revolt in your mind.' Gently he tipped up her face and mopped at her damp eyes with his handkerchief, then urged, 'Trust me, Jancis. Trust me and marry me.'

Her head went down, but his hand beneath her chin forced it up again so he could see into her eyes. But her look became shuttered. Now was the time to tell him that she couldn't marry him, couldn't marry him because there was not one solitary reason why he should have asked her to do so in the first place.

'I—I trust you,' she managed to tell him.

'And . . .' he prompted.

'And . . .' she began, but found she just couldn't tell him. Couldn't tell him and watch that carefully waiting expression he wore change to one of disgust. Particularly since she wanted to marry him above all else. 'Is Aileen Forbes in love with you?' she asked instead.

If it wasn't what he had been expecting to hear, then it didn't throw Thorp out of his stride. Without hesitation he answered, 'No. We've been—friends for some months now. But she was never in love with me.'

Jancis digested this, having to stamp down hard on giving her mind free range at the minute pause Thorp had given before bringing out the word 'friends'. She tried to oust jealousy, tried to think calmly. He was a grown man, for goodness' sake, and a monk's habit wouldn't have suited him anyway.

'Were . . .' She too had to pause before she asked her next question. 'Were,' she repeated, then changed it to are, 'Are you in love with her?'

'No, Jancis. I am not in love with her and never was.' He stopped to consider her seriously, that gentle note still in his voice, but a hardness lurking there when he added, 'So if that clears up all your questions—are you going to answer the one I've asked you?'

He meant was she going to marry him, she knew that. And may she be forgiven, she just couldn't tell him no.

'Yes,' she said, and wished that one word could have brought a smile to his face, but it didn't. 'Yes, Thorp, I will marry you.'

'Good,' he said, his tone even, then prevented her from saying anything else by suggesting, 'You're pretty emotionally used up. Why not go to bed and make an early night of it.' Then, obviously not expecting her to argue, he hesitated only briefly before, leaning down, he kissed her.

Jancis was on her way upstairs before she had time to think he hadn't given her a chance to respond to that lightest of kisses, but had promptly opened the door and pushed her through. He had said she was emotionally used up, and he was right. She just wasn't thinking as she floated along the landing to her room. She barely saw Sophie coming from the other direction.

'You've been crying,' Sophie accused when she was near enough to see her face.

'Have I?' Jancis replied, and without knowing it, opened her bedroom door.

About to follow her into her room, Sophie halted, her anxiety for her friend diminishing. Whatever had upset her, clearly Thorp had put right.

'Goodnight, Sophie,' said Jancis.

'Sleep well, Jancy,' Sophie said lightly, turning away with a shrug. Her look was knowing when she added, 'Pleasant dreams!'

Jancis lay in bed the next morning after a refreshing night's sleep, reminding herself of thoughts she'd had before sleep had claimed her. Until such time as Thorp showed signs of making concrete plans for their wedding day, she was going to hold back the truth from him. He was going to be livid when she told him, she didn't doubt that. But between now and then she was going to do all she could to get him to like her enough so that when she made her confession he would, she hoped, think twice about throwing her out on her ear.

Riding on optimism that if she could delay telling him, say, for a week, she might if she tried really hard even get him to fall a little bit in love with her, she went to the breakfast room to find Sophie had risen early and was there before her. And there she discovered she could say goodbye to all of her plans, because Sophie told her that after today Thorp wouldn't be around for a week or two.

'I got up especially early so that when Gareth arrived he should see me out for my usual morning stroll and feel obliged to give me a lift back to the house,' she complained, 'only to find Thorp had phoned him to get here straight away as there was some flap on.'

'Flap?' Jancis queried, hiding a smile at Sophie's strategy; it was the first early morning stroll she had heard of. Her smile faded when Sophie explained.

'Well, not flap exactly, I don't suppose Thorp has ever flapped in his life, but he received a call this morning about one of his experiments that had fouled up, and he's off to India before cockcrow tomorrow to look into it.'

'India!' Jancis exclaimed, ignoring the toast rack Sophie pushed under her nose, her appetite fast disappearing. Just thinking of not seeing Thorp for the week or two Sophie was explaining he could be gone for made her feel quite ill—how much worse it was going to be when she lost any right to see him at all.

'When I saw Gareth's car was already here I dared to poke my nose into the laboratory. Thorp,' said Sophie pouting, 'none too politely told me there were some tests they had to do that would keep them busy all day and they could do without my company. Still,' she added, brightening, 'with Thorp out of the country think of the opportunities I shall have!'

She beamed happily for some minutes, her heart obviously light as her mind thought of countless, casual of course, reasons for having to visit the laboratory. Then as though suddenly realising what Thorp's absence might mean to his fiancée:

'Oh, Jancy, I'm a selfish pig! You'll miss Thorp terribly, won't you?'

'Well——' began Jancis, then ceased prevaricating. 'Yes,' she said simply.

In bed that night she sat wide awake, wondering how it was possible to love someone so much that they occupied every waking thought, yet at the same time feel so angry with them that if Thorp's head came round her door now, she was sure it would take her all her time not to throw something at it.

Not once had she seen him today—well, not to talk to anyway. The glimpse she had caught of him had been as she had stood in the kitchen sharing a cup of tea with Mrs Hemmings. Her heart had lifted, then started to race when she saw him go by the window. He's coming in, she had thought, wondering if she looked all right. Was her hair right? Should she have worn a trouser suit rather than sweater and jeans? And then her heart had dipped, because Thorp hadn't come in. Casually, making sure he couldn't see her, she had edged to the kitchen window and saw that, as busy as he undoubtedly was that day, he still had time to spend a few moments chatting with Mr Hemmings who, his depression having taken an upswing, had been busy with his sketch pad for some time outside. Still hoping Thorp would come in when he had finished his conversation, Jancis felt her heart begin acting erratically again, only to slow down to a dull beat when she saw him striding over to the garages. From her vantage point she had seen him drive by in his car. He must need something urgently from town, she thought, something only he could go for too, since if he was so busy she would have thought he would have sent Gareth.

Strangely, as she couldn't help wondering if he might see Aileen Forbes in town, the thought didn't linger to wound her with that awful jealousy she found so nauseating. She trusted him. Somehow she knew if he did see her, then that meeting would be accidental.

But that had been then. Now, with the hands of her clock showing nearly eleven, no point in putting out the light as she was going to be awake for hours, that green-eyed monster began to get to her. She had seen nothing of him. Thorp hadn't even put in an appearance at dinner. She'd kill him if he'd gone to say goodbye to Aileen Forbes. He could go and see that woman, she fumed, but didn't have the courtesy to spare two minutes to tell his fiancée he was going away. She forgot entirely that she couldn't consider herself actually engaged to him since she had previously reasoned that he was going to nullify that state of affairs the moment he heard her confession.

The handle of her bedroom door turning alerted her to the fact that she was about to have company. It wouldn't be Sophie, because Sophie was in the habit of hurling herself in like a whirlwind. Her heart leapt that it might be Thorp, and her hostility against him melted, her anger disappeared, shyness taking its place as she pulled the covers up to her chin, all too conscious of her flimsy nightie. The door pushed inwards, and it was Thorp. Jancis swallowed several times while he half turned to close the door.

'All finished?' she enquired brightly, watching as he came over to the bed. There were lines of tiredness round his eyes and she felt a mean, short-tempered shrew that she had ever been angry with him for his neglect.

'Just.' He sat down on the edge of her bed, his grey

eyes full on her. She thought he was about to smile, then he observed the way she was hugging the covers to her and the smile didn't happen. 'I hoped you would still be awake,' he told her. 'I shall be away early and won't have another chance to see you.'

Her foolish heart began to dance as she put all sorts of meanings on that. Thorp had wanted to see her before he went. Surely that indicated that he liked her a little? She came down to earth with a bump to hear him say:

'I wanted to ask you if you could keep an eye on Sophie for me while I'm gone?'

Thank God for pride. 'Of course,' she replied, keeping her eyes veiled.

'Normally I'd hesitate to ask you to shoulder my responsibility. But it's important that I go to India, and Sophie does seem to have quietened down considerably since becoming infatuated with Gareth.'

'Yes, I think she has,' she inserted with an even politeness.

'You're so good for her,' Thorp went on, making her wonder if she had a label stuck on her that said. 'To be taken three times a day'. He turned the screw. 'Much more sensible,' he said. 'I don't think she'll do anything too outrageous,' he added, his voice taking on a light note, 'but if she does moot some plot such as shinning up the church tower and turning the weather vane north to south, do what you can to talk her out of it.'

Jancis allowed her lips to crack in a conventional smile. Then she watched, her heart leaden, as Thorp pushed his hand inside his trousers pocket to extract something.

'Would you wear this for me?' he asked, and so saying he took from the small square box she could now see he held, a magnificent emerald ring. In shock, forgetful of her flimsy attire, she let go the covers, stretching out a slender hand to hold the ring.

'It's beautiful!' she breathed, knowing she couldn't take

it, but feeling too choked at that moment to say so. Her eyes flicked from the ring to Thorp's face and she saw he looked pleased. And it was too much for her sensitivities just then to take that pleased look off his tired face by arguing that she couldn't possibly take anything so valuable.

'I'm glad you like it,' he said softly. 'With your eyes only an emerald would do, and since I wanted you to have it today, I was putting all my hopes on Todsbridge having what I wanted when I went into town.'

'Oh!' She was unable to stifle the exclamation, and had a real battle with tears as it came to her that, as busy as he had been that day, he had taken time off to go into town especially to get her an engagement ring.

A feeling of guilt swamped her. It was a beautiful ring, as she had said, but she had no entitlement to it. Had she known Thorp was going to buy it she would have stopped him. She should have stopped this whole thing last night, should have said 'No', not 'Yes' when he had asked her if she would marry him.

'Thorp,' she said hurriedly while the courage was about her. 'Thorp, I have to tell you . . .' but she got no farther.

'Aren't engagements supposed to be sealed with a kiss?' he interrupted, and before she could answer he had moved to gather her in his arms, and she was lost to rhyme or reason, had lost her basic instinct that knew right from wrong.

His kiss was gentle, unhurried, not designed to fully arouse her, but just having that physical contact with him had sensual delights rioting through her body. Thorp pulled back, but kept an arm around her shoulders.

'Aren't you going to put it on?' he asked.

'I—er——' she mumbled, confused from his kiss, wanting him to kiss her again. All thoughts of making her confession were mixed up in her mind. She wanted to put his ring on, if only for a moment. She knew he meant for it to go on her engagement finger, but she found, when all her emotions were begging for more than just kisses, she was just too shy to place the ring on that finger of her left hand.

'Here,' said Thorp, just as though he was aware of that particular shyness when all her other thoughts were so lacking in modesty. And he took hold of her left hand to slide the ring home on her engagement finger.

It looked so right there, she thought, awash with emotion. It fitted perfectly. Near to tears, she buried her head in his shoulder. If she spoke at all she just knew Thorp would know of her feelings for him. She felt his his arm tighten across her shoulders, naked except for two dainty shoulder straps, and raised her head to look at him. Then she wasn't sure who kissed first, but she was only aware it was all so right.

Perhaps Thorp hadn't intended to kiss her so thoroughly. Afterwards Jancis was certain she had felt him attempt to pull away. But just then her need for him had chased off any chance of sane thinking, and her arms were holding him, refusing to let him go, inviting him to stay.

'I must . . .' he began, then he groaned as though his will power was being torn assunder, and then everything was marvellous, for he was pushing her back against the pillows, his mouth on hers with a desperate kind of urgency.

Lost in an ardour that had her moaning for more, she wanted to feel him closer, much closer. And it was to her utter delight that she discovered Thorp felt the same, for, finding the bedclothes an encumbrance, he whipped them away, and a sigh of pure pleasure left her as she felt the hard length of his body against hers, her lips captured once more.

When even the way they were wasn't close enough for him and he released her to remove his sweater, she felt a fiery excitement shoot through her. Uncaring now that her nightdress left little to the imagination, she saw him look down at her curving body, saw his eyes flare as though the sight of her near nakedness inflamed him beyond endurance. Then his body was against hers again and this time he was kissing her and caressing her with an intimacy she had never before experienced, and she could only wonder at as her body rose in a tuneful crescendo of delight.

'Thorp!' she moaned his name, her hands roving freely over his bare chest. In ecstasy, she knew he would spend the night with her, and when a low groan emitted from him as his mouth left her by now naked breasts, she knew she would deny him nothing.

Why he moved just then she wasn't certain; probably to remove her nightdress altogether, she thought later. But as the terrifying thought came that he was going to leave her, like this, the words panicked to her lips with nothing she could do to stop them.

'Don't go,' she begged. 'Oh, Thorp, please—please stay!'

At that moment all her senses, her emotions, that deeply-lying sensuality hinted at with Shaw but untapped until the man she really loved had kissed her, knew no reason to withhold anything. But her voice, fluttering with panic, had Thorp pulling away from her.

His face was flushed, as she suspected was hers. His breathing was ragged, a glazed look in his eyes. He seemed to her then to be a man fighting desperately to get on top of the passion that had raged between them. Bewildered, she felt him forcibly push her hands from him, then he took a harsh grating breath, and as though she had been struck Jancis saw him haul himself of the bed and reach for his sweater.

He's not staying! He's going to leave! she thought, not believing it. She saw him shrug into his sweater, caught sight of her own near naked body, the pleading words she had uttered bounced back in her ears, and her pride was mortified with shame.

With shaking hands she dragged the covers up over her. And now, far from being so much in love with him that nothing mattered, she hated him with everything in her being, that he could spurn her, could take her along that heady path and leave her to find her own way back.

'Jancy,' he said, the first time he had called her Jancy, and her name left him on a sound as ragged as his breathing.

'I hate you!' she stormed, careless that not too long ago she had been showing that hate in a very odd way. She was riding on pride, she didn't want to hear anything he had to say. 'Leave,' she ordered. 'Go to India. Go to India and don't bother to come back!'

Her tears had already started when she turned over and buried her face in her pillow. Oh God, she prayed, make him go before the sobs that were building up inside started to rack her.

She heard a movement that told her Thorp was near, and held herself tense, her teeth in the pillow, when she thought his hand touched her hair. And then, as if he knew how much she hated him, how much he would be wasting his time if he said anything, he moved again, and the next sound Jancis heard was that of him going over to the door, opening it and closing it quietly after him.

CHAPTER TEN

SOMETHING hard pressing against her cheek brought Jancis up from an exhausted sleep. She pulled her hand away from her face and saw the emerald Thorp had given her.

'Oh God,' she groaned, as full remembrance crashed in. She had no more tears to cry, and it was as useless now as it had been last night to question what had got into her that left no room for well brought up reservations. She didn't hate Thorp, and love made a nonsense of propriety.

He had asked her to keep an eye on Sophie while he was away, so she would have to stay, but she wouldn't wear his ring; she had no right to it. But before she could remove it from her finger ready for its return the next time she saw him, Sophie in her usual manner came bursting in.

'Jan . . .' she began, and stopped dead. 'Oh, your poor swollen eyes!' she sympathised, and coming nearer the bed, 'Never mind, love, he'll soon be back.' Then catching sight of her ring, 'Yoicks! When old Thorp falls, he falls with a bang, doesn't he?'

Sighing inwardly, Jancis knew the ring would have to remain on her finger. She just wasn't up to removing it and then explaining everything to Sophie. And anyway, since she was sure Sophie had a fair idea of her feelings for Thorp, she just didn't dare risk Sophie inadvertently giving her away before she could leave. Thorp knew she wasn't immune to him, but . . . Oh God!

Thorp wasn't exactly immune to her either, she got round to thinking a couple of days later. Up until then her feelings of hurt had been edged with a feeling of guilt that the whole mess was her fault.

As the days wore on, tired with the self-inflicted punishment of her thoughts, she came out of her mood of despondency to feel the aggression stirring. She hadn't asked him to come to her room, had she? She wasn't the one who had kissed first. He had started it all by kissing her.

Another couple of days went by and with them her spurt of anger. Thorp hadn't kissed her with passion when he had put that ring on her finger. He had tried to break away, and, she groaned, what had she done but clung on to him?

Anger was back two days later. A fine fiancé he was! Away over a week and not so much as a phone call. True, Gareth had said Thorp was in a region where trans-continental communication might be difficult, not to say impossible, but that was only a small matter. She wasn't prepared to make excuses for him, even if her last words to him could have given him the impression she wouldn't care if she never saw him again.

As the time neared when any day could bring Thorp home, Jancis was forced to face up to the fact that she wasn't his fiancée anyway. Oh, she might be wearing his ring, but the time would shortly be here when all that would be ended. Unable to bear the see-sawing of her emotions, she had decided that at the first opportunity she was going to come clean.

Although it seemed to her that all her thinking had been given over to thoughts of Thorp, that wasn't strictly true, she realised twelve days after he had gone and she sat eating lunch with Sophie. She and Sophie had taken Mr Hemmings with them when they had gone to the vil-lage a couple of times. And yesterday she had spent ages talking to him and Mrs Hemmings in the kitchen while Sophie had been 'helping' Gareth in the laboratory.

'Do you mind eating dinner by yourself tonight?' Sophie

asked, licking her lips after polishing off one of her favourite puddings that Mrs Hemmings had made specially for her.

'Thinking of going out?' Jancis asked warily. One never knew with Sophie.

'Sort of.' A gleam appeared in Sophie's eyes. 'Gareth has an experiment he's working on which he doesn't want to leave until it's completed. That means he'll be working late tonight.'

'So you're skipping dinner to go and help him?'

Sophie shook her head. 'Actually I think I'm more of a hindrance than a help, though Gareth is too much of a gentleman to say so. No, the thing is, since Mrs Hemmings will be making dinner for Gareth anyway I suggested he came and had dinner with us.'

For a moment Jancis was mystified, then she thought daylight was beginning to come through. 'You mean you'd like me to have dinner in my room—have a sudden indisposition or something so you and Gareth can dine alone?'

'No, dope,' said Sophie, laughing. 'Gareth says he can't leave his experiment and intends to munch while he's working. So I rather thought since the small table in the laboratory is going to be laid for one, it might just as well be laid for two.'

'And what does Gareth think about that?' Jancis asked, unable to hold back a grin. When Sophie went after something, then heaven help the poor victim!

'He doesn't know yet,' said Sophie happily. Then thoughtfully, 'If you don't mind, though, I think I'll tell him I was lonesome on my own since you had a sudden bilious attack and went to bed minus dinner, plus sleeping pill.'

It was the following Monday before Thorp returned after being away for nearly three weeks. Sophie, since she appeared to be getting nowhere with Gareth, had now changed tactics and was exercising every restraint and playing it cool. She and Jancis had been for a walk, and though the route they had taken didn't touch the laboratory, Sophie suggested they should detour that way back so that should Gareth be watching, he would see when she didn't go in that she was ignoring him. They were passing the laboratory when on being requested by Sophie to look at the windows to see if Gareth was watching, Jancis saw, with an acceleration of heartbeats, not Gareth, but Thorp.

'Thorp's back!' Sophie whooped, having had to look at the windows despite herself, and forgetful for a moment his return could be limiting if she again decided to change tactics. Then, as though expecting Jancis to be right behind her, she wheeled off towards the laboratory door.

She turned at the door to see Jancis hadn't moved. 'Aren't you coming?' Jancis shook her head. Just the sight of Thorp, and her plans for what she had to tell him became tangled. She needed time to compose herself before she told him anything. 'Poor Jancy,' Sophie gave her a sympathetic grin. 'You won't be as shy as this with him after you're married!'

Jancis hurried indoors, wishing she could be again the girl she had been, the girl who seldom cried. Even after Shaw she had not been so constantly battling against tears. 'After you're married!' she thought, and was fighting tears again. There would be no chance of marriage with Thorp once she had told him everything.

On her way to her room it came to her that Sophie was bound to have told Thorp she was aware he was home, for he had been in conversation with Gareth and hadn't seen her. Wouldn't it be expected of him to come looking for her? Wouldn't he, just for the look of it, leave the laboratory to come and say hello? Her steps halted. He might even take it into his head to seek her out in her bedroom if he couldn't find her downstairs.

Hastily she turned about and made for the drawing

room. If her supposition was right and he did come looking for her, she didn't want any conversation with him in her bedroom. It was there she had last seen him, there that in her anguish she had told him she hated him.

Feeling unbearably hot at just the thought of seeing him, with shaking fingers she slipped off the jacket she had on over her sweater and trousers; and then she heard the front door open. She knew it wasn't Sophie following her in, the tread was firm, less hurried. She was facing the door when Thorp walked in dressed in a well fitting suit of light grey, and her heart flipped over at just seeing him.

He stood looking intently at her, a suggestion of a smile on his face. But when without a word he moved and looked like coming over to her, she was so afraid he might think it was his right to kiss her in greeting—though perhaps he wouldn't, since he must remember she had said she hated him—she thought, already confused just by having him in the same room, that she moved too—moved in the opposite direction away from him. She was too well aware of the havoc he could cause if he took it into his head to take her in his arms. All the carefully rehearsed things she had planned to say to him would be just so much jibbering jumble if she felt that warm mouth against her own.

'Er—hello,' she said, when Thorp stopped and didn't look like coming any nearer. And for her pains she felt all sorts of an idiot. What sort of a greeting was that, for goodness' sake! 'Did you have a—a good trip?'

'Most satisfactory,' he said, and just hearing his voice after over two weeks' absence was like music in her ears.

He was watching her carefully, she knew that. She hadn't missed that his eyes had gone to her left hand to see if she was wearing his ring. It reminded her, though she needed very little reminding, since it had been her constant thought since he had been away, of what she had to do.

'You were able to—er—sort out the problem?' she asked, her voice sounding stilted in her own ears; lord knew what Thorp was making of it.

'Yes,' he said briefly, not explaining the technicalities which would have meant nothing to her anyway. 'How about you?' he asked slowly, and she knew then he had discerned that she was as jumpy as a kitten. 'Have you any problems, Jancis?'

'No,' she said, and groaned inwardly that she wasn't more sophisticated as she amended it to, 'I mean yes, but—but if you've only just arrived home my problems can wait.'

Coward, she called herself. Oh God, what a yellow-streaked coward she was! It was no good saying she wouldn't have been so cowardly if she didn't love him. Dear God, he was the answer to all her prayers, dreams, hopes, and she was going to have to tell him something that would have all her hopes of being married to him so much nothing.

She saw him hesitate as though he agreed that he didn't want to know what her problems were. And then as he turned and she thought he was going to leave, it was as though the state her nerves were in had him against his better judgment changing his mind, because he turned back to face her.

'You'd better tell me what it is that's worrying you,' he said shortly, his tone not very inviting.

'It can wait,' Jancis hedged. He'd flay her alive with his tongue if she told him while he was in this mood, she thought, shying away, all her resolves to tell him at the first opportunity fast disappearing.

'Spit it out, Jancis,' he told her roughly, 'I've got work to do.'

'I can't marry you.' The words left her bluntly, rocketing out, fired by his rough attitude.

Thorp put more space between them and went to stare

out of the window, his hands thrust deeply into his trouser pockets.

'You think you still hate me because I made you feel like a woman.' he said curtly.

'No,' came from her before she could stop it, and her creamy complexion was a heated scarlet when he turned to look at her. 'I—you—well, that has nothing to do with it.'

'So,' he drawled, his eyes steady on her face, 'the reason you feel you can't marry me isn't that my lovemaking offends you?'

'No,' she mumbled, lowering her head. She wished he hadn't started on about the last time she had seen him because remembering those dizzying, sense-taking moments in his arms was making her want to be in his arms again, was clouding her vision.

'In that case I think we're off to a flying start, don't you?'

'Yes—No.' Did every girl in love have moments of difficulty with her own language? she wondered, not sure what she wanted to say any more; she had already told him she thought there was more to marriage than sex.

Thorp smiled as though divining her last thought, then ignoring completely that she had just stated she couldn't marry him, he said gently, 'We could have a good marriage, Jancis. I know you've been bruised by that other relationship you had and I can understand your nervousness.' She tried to keep her face deadpan; her reasons for saying she couldn't marry him had nothing to do with Shaw. 'But you and I both hold the same views on fidelity. I shall never let you down. Trust me, I . . .'

'Oh, but I do trust you,' broke from her. 'But . . .'

'But you're unsure of this step we're about to take?' He smiled again, encouragingly this time. 'Have no fears, my dear,' he said, and that 'my dear' had her not fearing anything save that she was going to melt in a heap at his feet if he went on in this gentle way. 'I know this marriage is right for us.'

He sounded convinced, but he didn't know what she had to tell him yet. About to gather all her courage and tell him now before her desire to be married to him overrode every other consideration, Jancis opened her mouth to tell him, only to find he had got in first.

'Perhaps it would help you to realise how important our marriage is to me if I tell you . . .' He stopped as though making an unaccustomed search for the right words, and suddenly Jancis felt as though she was on the edge of a precipice.

Was he going to tell her he loved her a little? Oh God, could he? Did he? He looked so serious, she thought, her heart beating so wildly she felt it would jump out of her body. She could be insanely wrong, the thought clashed, and just in case she was, she tilted her chin ready for the blow, keeping her face impassive.

Thorp studied the aloofness of her expression for a moment, then went on slowly, 'My father left me an inheritance that precludes me from being a lifelong bachelor. I'm duty bound to marry some time if only to ensure that the works of art and fine properties left to me are handed down.'

'Oh!' Being dumped in a bath of cold water had nothing on the terrible dashing of her ridiculous hopes that drenched her with his words. What an idiot she was! But pride demanded that she kept him from seeing how let down she felt as she sought round in the boggle of her mind for some way to reply. 'You mean for the sake of an—an heir, you want—need—to be married?'

'That's right,' he nodded calmly. 'I should very much like you to be my wife, Jancis.'

'Oh,' she said again, and her heart, having dropped, now picked up its wild beat again. She could still marry him if she wished. 'Why me particularly?' she asked, her insides churning.

'Why not you? You're beautiful, intelligent, besides which, we're half way there already.'

That was a cruel reminder that she was the instigator, by her actions, of the beginning of this marriage talk. Had thinking himself obliged to marry her triggered off those thoughts about needing an heir? Oh God, she suddenly thought, as far as Thorp was concerned, she might be on the way to producing an heir already.

'I'm not!' flew from her before she calmed down at the alert look that brought to his face. 'Thorp, I'm not—er—pregnant after all.' Her cheeks coloured as that confession was torn from her and she turned away from him. Then she nearly jumped out of her skin, for he had moved so silently she hadn't heard him and had come to stand behind her, his hands coming to rest on her shoulders.

'Well, I'm not in too much of a hurry,' he said, then softly, 'Would you mind being pregnant by me, Jancis?' Too choked to speak, blindly she shook her head, and in that movement he seemed to read that she had no further objections, for he said, 'That's settled, then,' just as though it was.

And it was settled, she thought a second later, because nothing now would have her repeating the words, 'I can't marry you,' because she wanted to marry him so much, loved him so much, surely it couldn't be wrong? She would be a good wife to him, bear his children . . .

'Sophie's parents are due home next Monday,' he broke into her thoughts, his voice becoming businesslike. 'Can you be ready to marry me the following Friday?'

'A week on Friday!' she exclaimed, spinning round, finding she was still in his firm hold but now had the added complication of being pinned by his grey eyes.

'I said I was in no hurry to make you pregnant,' he said, refusing to let her look away at the intimacy of this talk, 'but I am in a hurry to have you in my bed.'

'You are?' A thrill of excitement took over, which made her say without thinking, 'But-but I thought you didn't want . . . I mean when you left me that . . .'

'The night before I went away,' he finished for her, and now his eyes were showing a warm look. 'If you thought I didn't want you desperately that night, Jancis Langfield, then you just don't know as much about men as you thought you did, do you?'

She had known he had desired her, of course she had known that. But she had thought his desire couldn't have been so all-consuming as her need for him, for she had thought they had both been at the point of no return, past it, when he had controlled his desire and pulled away from her.

Thorp broke off his teasing to sit down with her, and became businesslike again as he told her of the arrangements he would make for their wedding. A shade bewildered, Jancis listened, feeling breathless that once Thorp made up his mind to anything, he didn't hang about.

William wouldn't be able to come to the wedding, she told him, trying hard to concentrate when he asked who she would like to be there. 'And I don't think my father will want to come.' Rarely seeing her father, she had grown apart from him, not that they had ever been very close. 'My mother lives in Switzerland now,' she added quietly. 'I don't know if it will be convenient for her to come either.'

She felt regretful about that. Of late she had found herself more in sympathy with her mother than she had ever done since finding out that she too could be unfaithful. She must have had a terrible life with her father.

'Does it upset you that your mother might not be able to make it?' Thorp asked, noticing that she had looked solemn for a moment.

'It would have been nice,' she understated, trying to

make her voice off hand. The sort of wedding Thorp was planning was just a necessary chore to be got out of the way before they started living together, she suspected. She didn't want to give him any idea what her wedding would mean to her, or how lovely it would be if her mother could be there. As it was, she was hoping he was believing she had agreed to marry him because after Shaw—an idea Thorp himself had put into her mind—her faith in men had been shattered, and that she wanted a marriage where she could be sure her partner felt the same way as she did about the sanctity of marriage vows.

It was too much to expect that their plans could be made uninterrupted. Sophie suddenly burst in, her eyes shining, breaking into their conversation without apology.

'Can Gareth have the day off tomorrow?' she asked Thorp. 'He's going to ask you himself, but I just couldn't bear it if you said no.'

'Far be it from me to be the one to take those stars out of your eyes,' Thorp answered sardonically. 'You've got him on his starting blocks, then?' he added, the corner of his mouth turning up in a grin before he came over the guardian uncle. 'Where is he thinking of taking you— or to rephrase that, where are you thinking of taking him?'

'We're going on a picnic,' said Sophie, sublimely happy.

That tomorrow was the first of February and that the weather was hardly picnicking weather hadn't passed Thorp by. 'Sophie,' he said, his voice half teasing, 'do me a favour—try not to make Gareth as feather-brained as yourself.'

Sophie grinned, not at all put out. Then Thorp turned to Jancis, his look reminding her of something they had discussed a few minutes earlier.

'Er—there's a favour I'd like to ask you to do me too, Sophie, if you wouldn't mind.'

'Anything,' said Sophie promptly, God in her heaven, all right with her world, then seeing Jancis seemed a little nervous of asking the favour, 'Anything, Jan,' she said, her face sobering. 'You know that.'

'Would you be my bridesmaid a week this Friday?' she asked with a tentative smile, and was nearly flattened as with a yelp Sophie hurled herself between her and Thorp on the settee to give her a hug.

Jancis had not given thought to the exact location for their marriage ceremony, but when Thorp asked her the next day, the house strangely peaceful without Sophie, if she had any preference, she answered, quite without thinking:

'There's an old church at Little Bramington that's really quite beautiful,' and then quickly, not wanting him to see it would matter very much if she could be married to him in the church she had known for most of her life, 'But that's impossible isn't it,' and making her voice light, 'It doesn't matter to me where we marry, actually.'

But it seemed that Thorp didn't recognise the word impossible. In no time he had been in touch with the vicar—still the same one she knew, Mr Exton—and all the arrangements were made.

Sophie, when she came home, her eyes sparkling after what she described as a fabulous day out with Gareth, squeaked with delight and doubly endorsed Thorp's view that her parents would be delighted to have her married from their home.

'They'll be mortally offended if you don't,' she added. 'They were always fond of you, Jancy, and I could make a record of the times they've said after I've taken some of my other friends home, "Why can't you take up with someone nice like Jancis Langfield?"'

Jancis had to laugh as Sophie imitated her mother's severest tones. But as the next couple of days passed, and the day of her wedding drew nearer, she began to feel unsettled, began to experience doubts she didn't want to feel.

It would have helped, she thought, if she could see more of Thorp, had some chance of getting to know him better before the wedding. He was busy, she knew that. They were going to honeymoon on an island in the Seychelles, which meant, of course, that he had to take time off from his work, and she understood that with him going to India so unexpectedly, he probably had a lot of catching up to do as well as try and get everything in order before they went. But it seemed to her that he was positively avoiding her as Wednesday and Thursday came and went with her barely seeing anything of him. Didn't he want to marry her after all? she even thought at one point when he had passed her in the hall on the way to his study. She had been looking her best too; she was wearing the plum velvet and had spent ages with her hair. And all Thorp had done was pause for a moment, his eyes going over her, then with his face quite expressionless he had said evenly, 'I won't be able to join you for dinner,' and then muttered something about pressing paper work before he had gone on his way.

They had come near to having a row too when on Friday, with her wedding only a week away, Jancis told him she was returning to her flat tomorrow.

'What the hell for!' he had bitten at her, not at all in the way she thought a man would if he was looking forward to being married. It was one of the few times they had been alone together having dinner. Sophie, to use her own words, had got Gareth to take her to the cinema in Todsbridge.

'Well, I've got my clothes to see to, for one thing,' Jancis answered, feeling on the defensive and not liking it. 'And masses of things to do besides,—and anyway,' she added, her aggression rising since Thorp continued to glower at her. 'Sophie will be leaving herself on Monday.'

'And you think it isn't the done thing for you to be

alone under my roof with only Mrs Hemmings to chaperone you,' he said, quite nastily, she thought. 'My God, do you think I'm going to sneak into your room one night and rape you?'

'No, I don't!' flew from her, anger jetting it to the surface. If she had given a thought to being alone with him under his roof, it was only to wonder what they would have to say to each other without Sophie there as a buffer. Lord, she couldn't help the thought, and she was thinking of marrying him!

She forced herself to be calm, her plans to try and make him fall in love with her taking a severe blow. For heaven help her, she still did want to marry him.

'Nothing in my wardrobe is suitable to be married in,' she said, striving to take the heat out of her voice. 'I shall need time to look round for something.'

'Todsbridge shopping centre not good enough for you?' he asked coldly, and she wondered how many stitches he would need if she gave in to the violent urge to throw the coffee pot at his head.

'Oh—go to hell!' she shouted stormily, and was on her feet making for the door before he caught her and hauled her up short.

'Don't you . . .' he began aggressively, a look of pure fury on his face when he spun her round to face him. And then he saw the tears shimmering in her eyes, and the fury in him died as though it had never been.

'Jancis,' he breathed softly, his hands tightening on her arms, then as he recovered his equilibrium, one corner of his mouth went up in that tantalising lopsided grin she loved so much, as he confessed, 'You delight my home so much I'd been thinking it would only have to be without your beauty for one night—the night before our wedding.'

Her heart was hammering, her love for him uppermost that if perhaps it wasn't him she delighted so much, then at least he was saying he liked to have her about the place.

'I'm sorry I told you to go to hell,' she said huskily. 'I think those pre-marriage nerves everyone talks about must be getting to me.' She smiled at him, a smile of genuine warmth and charm, and abruptly Thorp let her go.

'Let me know what time you want to leave tomorrow. I'll drive you.'

Hurt by his sudden cold change of manner, Jancis cancelled the, 'You don't have to bother, I can easily catch a train' and amended it to a formal, 'Thank you,' and left him.

Since Gareth had told Sophie he would be away for the weekend and there was no chance of her seeing him, Sophie elected to go to London with them.

'I could stay overnight, Jancy,' she offered, 'and bring as many of your things as I can manage back to the Manor in my car on Sunday.'

Jancis fell in with the idea, not suggesting as had occurred to her that she stay two days and go from her flat direct to her parents' home, knowing that if at all possible Sophie was hoping to see Gareth again before she returned to Little Bramington on Monday. Love got you like that, she thought disconsolately. Thorp might be impossible to live with at times, but he was also impossible to live without. It would be almost a whole week before she saw him again. It was going to seem like a year.

Thorp didn't stay any longer at her flat than to have a cup of tea, Mrs Hemmings having thought to press a bottle of milk into her hands as they were leaving. Never was Jancis more glad of Sophie's bubbling chatter as the three of them sat in her flat. She was on edge with Thorp, she knew it. She wanted to feast her eyes on him, for soon he would be going, but she was afraid to give him more than the occasional glance lest he read in her look that he hadn't gone yet and already she was on the brink of pining for him. When he stood up to leave, her heart sagged.

'I'll see you to the door,' she offered politely, and saw Sophie smile, knowing she was thinking they would be some time out in the hall where she wouldn't be able to see their passionate parting.

Thankful Sophie hadn't got X-ray eyes, Jancis stood in the hall with Thorp, the door to the sitting room closed.

'I don't think I shall be able to get to town to see you before Friday,' he said, his hand already on the door as though he couldn't wait to leave.

She had never supposed that he would. 'That's all right,' she said carefully. 'I have simply masses to do anyway.'

'Until Friday, then,' said Thorp, the door open.

Until Friday, she was silently echoing, a hurt aching inside her that he could sound so casual. Then just at that moment he turned his head to look at her, then suddenly the door was slammed shut and she was in his arms.

Instantly her misery vanished, her arms went up and around him and she clung to him as he was clutching her to him. But before he made any attempt to kiss her, the door to the sitting room opened and there was Sophie.

'Oh, sorry,' she said, 'I thought I heard you leave.'

'You always were the most untimely brat,' Thorp told his niece, letting go of Jancis, then ignoring Sophie, he gently touched his fiancée's cheek.

'Until Friday, Jancis,' he said.

'Until Friday, Thorp,' she managed, then he was gone.

While Sophie was with her she had little chance to think over that unexpected embrace he had given her. She and Sophie spent the rest of Saturday emptying wardrobes and drawers and coming to the conclusion that several trips in the Morgan would be needed for all the stuff that had to be transported.

'You and Thorp can see to the rest of the gear when you come back from your honeymoon,' Sophie opined, showing a practical side to her nature that was rarely seen. 'After all, until you and William decide what you want to do about the flat there's no hurry, is there?' and with her head on one side, 'If I hadn't met Gareth I'd have begged you to let me rent it from you and tried to make the parents see what a good idea it was, but—funny, isn't it, how your whole way of thinking changes when you're in love.'

'How are things going with you and Gareth?' Jancis asked gently.

'In a word, slow, but I'm working on it,' Sophie replied, then, her face brightening, 'I say, Jancy, can I come and stay with you after your honeymoon?'

When Sophie had gone, Jancis had too much time in which to do her private thinking. Sophie was coming again on Tuesday and they were both going to search the shops for 'something that'll knock 'em in the aisles', according to Sophie—who, since she had helped Jancis pack her pretty but in her opinion definitely not honeymoon lingerie, said she would again stay overnight on Tuesday so they could shop the next day for something a bit more imaginative.

The joy that had surged through her when Thorp had clutched her to him in the hall had by now evaporated as she tormented herself with thoughts of the way he had been with her up until then.

On Monday the doubt again returned—did Thorp really want to marry her? It had her so churned up she almost rang him to ask him just that very question. Her hand even went so far as to pick up the phone, but her fingers froze and she couldn't dial his number. What if he said, 'No, I don't want to marry you'? Instead she dialled her father's number and was soon talking to the man who had more smooth charm than fidelity. She told him she was getting married on Friday and asked if he could be there.

'Married?' Tarquin Langfield exclaimed. 'Friday—this Friday?' and she could almost see him wincing at the idea of having a daughter old enough to be married. 'And where exactly is this event to take place?'

Jancis put down the phone, not sure whether she was glad or sorry her father wouldn't be there. Little Bramington had done it, of course. Her father wouldn't be seen dead in the place. It must have dug a hole in his vanity, not merely pricked it that her mother had made him lose face in the village. Still, he could have shown enough interest in her to ask who his future son-in-law was to be.

The phone still in her hand, she made a call to Switzerland. But she was out of luck there as she was informed by her mother's housekeeper that her mother was in St Moritz and wasn't expected back for two weeks.

She cheered up when Sophie arrived early the next day. 'Mother's positively off her trolley with delight about you and Thorp,' Sophie told her before she had so much as removed her driving gloves. 'I arrived home about half an hour before the parents and stopped Mother's "What have you been up to while we've been away?" inquisition mid-gallop when I told her you and Thorp were getting married. She was on the phone to him before I'd finished. Incidentally, she says it's unthinkable that you stay here until Thursday, and that if we can get all our shopping done today, then you're to come home with me tonight.'

Jancis answered her noncommittally. But as they darted in and out of shops, finding the simple white dress and white hat that was just exactly right in the second shop, though having to search a little farther for the dress Sophie was to wear, Jancis came round to the view that since she felt so much more cheerful now that she had Sophie for company, she would much rather be in Little Bramington than stay in her flat and lacerate herself with those night-marish doubts.

They were both exhausted when, armed with countless carrier bags housing not only their dresses, but shoes to go with them, they arrived back at the flat. Pushed into the lingerie department of one store while Sophie left her to go and have a cup of coffee on the top floor, Jancis had been unable to resist buying some of the frothy chiffon and lace on display.

'Phew!' exclaimed Sophie, her shoes already off. 'Go and make a cup of tea, Jancy, there's a dear. I swear I can't go another step until my feet have cooled down!'

Thus instructed, Jancis went to make the tea, to return with the tray to hear Sophie announce, 'Right, we'll drain the pot, then head for the outback. I'll ring Mother and tell her we'll be home in time for dinner.'

Because it was what she wanted to do, Jancis didn't argue, and in no time it seemed Sophie was driving along in front with her following behind in her car loaded with the purchases of the day plus her suitcases. Then before she knew it she was passing through the well remembered village of Little Bramington, past her old home, and pulling on to the drive of the house some way past it. And barely had she got out of the car than Sophie's mother and father were there, Mrs Ellington putting her arms around her and hugging her as if she was some long-lost relative and making Jancis want to cry, she was so welcoming.

'It's so good of you to have me, Mrs Ellington,' she said, only to have her thanks brushed aside as Mrs Ellington, about eight or nine years older than Thorp, told her she would have to try and get into the habit of calling her Paula now that they were to be sisters-in-law.

'Dan,' said Mr Ellington, beaming at her, his blue eyes so like Sophie's and looking just as full of mischief as his greeting followed his wife's. 'Daniel will do if it's too much of a transition all at once. Though Paula only ever calls me Daniel when it's wrist-slapping time!'

After such a lovely welcome, it wasn't until she lay in her bed that night, the house quiet, that the worries she had hoped left behind in London came again to torment her. Was she doing the right thing? she asked herself again. She didn't doubt *she* wanted to marry Thorp. The idea of being his wife was all-consuming. But was marriage to her right for *him*? Wasn't she being utterly selfish in wanting to tie him to her for ever? Thorp had the same feelings about fidelity as she did. He had told her so. Marriage for him meant the same as it did for her. It meant a total commitment, a vow never to be broken. Oh God, she groaned, thinking she would go mad, did all brides feel like this?

CHAPTER ELEVEN

It was to take until Thursday, the evening before her wedding, before Jancis got to the root cause of what was really troubling her. Over the past forty-eight hours she had wrestled too many times with the thought that for a man who had declared how desperately he had wanted her that night, Thorp had not once since that night kissed her. Was that the sign of a man with a desperate need for her?

More than once she thought she would go mad with the punishment of her thoughts—thoughts that again gnawed at her as up in her room that night she prepared to change ready to go down to dinner.

Her hand on the wardrobe door ready to take out the dress she would wear, she wondered again why, if Thorp was as keen to make love to her as he had said, he should be so lacking in ardency? What held him back? As far as he knew he had already been her lover, so . . .

Her breath was suddenly sucked in to leave her on a strangled gasp. Oh God, she hadn't told him! As far as Thorp knew he had already been her lover. She felt the colour drain from her.

Blindly she stumbled away from the wardrobe, groping for the bed, needing something solid beneath her to sit on. How had she got as far as her wedding eve without telling him? What had she been thinking about? Thorp had said marriage for him was unthinkable without trust and fidelity.

Her mind became besieged with thoughts she didn't want, but which had to be faced. He had to know—had to know she had lied to him, had to know he hadn't so much as made contact with any part of her that night. She had been off the bed before his attempt to grab her could be achieved. Oh God, she groaned. Thorp had to be told, and told before tomorrow.

Apart from his own strongly held views on keeping faith, her own deep-rooted sense of what was right was plaguing her. Had been plaguing her for over a week now, she realised, only she hadn't recognised it for what it was. How could she go to him in marriage with that lie, that broken trust, between them? Yet would he want to marry her when he knew?

Sophie bursting in had her white strained face turning to the door. 'I've just . . .' Sophie broke off. 'Jancy!' she exclaimed, hurrying over to her. 'Whatever's the matter? You look ghastly!'

'I . . . I've got to see Thorp,' Jancy whispered, the truth of that hitting her as the words she was barely conscious of uttering sounded back in her ears.

'Thorp!' Sophie exclaimed, startled. "What . . .'

'I must see him, Sophie,' she said, then realising Sophie was looking distressed, made an effort to pull herself together. 'I can't explain, Sophie, but I must see him.'

Sophie proved then she had come a long way since she had fallen in love with Gareth Logan, from being the harebrained girl she had been, though she would never be anything than the totally warmth-giving creature she was.

'Shall I ring him for you and ask him to come over?' she suggested, sensing an emergency and not questioning her friend's need to see her fiancé.

'No!' Jancis said more sharply than she meant. 'I'll go and see him.'

Sophie bit back the protest that came to her lips. 'Are you sure, Jan? You don't look fit to drive,' she said doubtfully.

'I must.' She wanted to be on her way, wanted to go

now. She had to see him without delay.

Dressed as she was in jeans and a shirt, she hurriedly left the bed, opened the wardrobe and was blinded for a moment by her wedding dress, She reached inside for her sheepskin jacket, then turned to a troubled-looking Sophie.

'Would you explain to your parents for me?' she asked, hoping not to see anyone on her way out. Her journey was urgent and though she knew she owed Paula and Dan Ellington an explanation, she just couldn't face it.

'Sure,' said Sophie, seeing she was determined, and forcing a smile, 'Drive carefully, love.'

Jancis turned into the drive of Widefields Manor three quarters of an hour later, knowing that since she was a fairly steady driver she must have driven with all due caution, but having no recollection of braking, changing gear or stopping at traffic lights. There was an emptiness gnawing away at her insides which had nothing to do with the fact that she had skipped dinner.

She left the car and went up the stone steps to ring the bell, praying Thorp was in. She had to see him if it meant waiting for hours, though she thought she would grow demented if she had to wait very long. If he told her to get lost when he heard what she had to say she just didn't know how she was going to get back to Little Bramington. Paula had to be considered; she would have to tell her, since she had organised such a splendid wedding breakfast, that the wedding was off.

She heard footsteps coming along the hall, and for the first time in her life had to fight with all she knew not to run away. She could still marry him, called a tempting voice as she waited for Mrs Hemmings to open the door, but that voice was trampled on as the word 'fidelity' flattened it.

It was with fresh shock that she saw it wasn't Mrs Hemmings who opened the door. Thorp stood there, big, dark and with the light behind him. What he could see in her face she couldn't tell, but from his face she could read nothing.

'Come in,' he invited after a long moment when she thought she was going to have her conversation with him on the doorstep. His voice was even, not surprised as she had thought it would be since she was supposed to be safely ensconced in his sister's home.

Frozen, she couldn't move—until Thorp's hand came out and prompted her over the threshold. Still with his hand on her arm, he led her into the drawing room, helping her off with her jacket without saying a word. He then, still unspeaking, urged her to be seated, then left her on the settee to go over to the drinks table where he poured two drinks.

'Drink this,' he said, coming back to her and giving her one of the glasses.

'I don't—want a drink,' she said, more eager to get what she had to say over and done than to observe the niceties.

'You look as though you could do with one,' he said calmly, and because he seemed to be expecting it of her, Jancis took a sip and realised he had given her brandy, when he knew very well that drink wasn't her first preference.

She knew then that he was aware of her semi-shocked state and quickly took another sip before setting the glass down on the table nearby, watching as Thorp took the seat opposite and knocked back his drink in one as though he needed it.

Realising it was up to her to tell him what she was doing here, because for all he wasn't asking, he could have no idea, she cleared her throat nervously.

'I—er—had to see you, Thorp,' she began.

'It couldn't wait until tomorrow?'

'No,' she agreed, 'it couldn't wait.'

'I'm sorry to hear that.'

His voice sounded level, but there was something in it that had her head coming up. She looked across at him and thought he had lost some of his colour, but didn't have time to dwell on the thought because he was saying:

'So you have come to tell me you can't go through with it. That you don't want to marry me after all?' His voice wasn't level any more, there was a rough aggression to it that had her growing agitated.

'No—yes, I mean . . .'

'I thought we'd had this discussion before,' he challenged harshly. 'I thought we'd both agreed that trust and faith in each other mattered above most things.' He was leaning forward in his aggression, his face cold with anger. 'Yet with our wedding only fourteen hours away you take it into your head to break your promise to me.'

'I'm not . . .' she began, but wasn't allowed to go on.

'You're not!' Thorp repeated, his anger with her not letting up. 'Then why the hell *are* you here if it isn't to tell me . . .'

'I . . . I . . .' his anger was unnerving her. God, she thought, he'd probably strangle her when he heard her out! If his patience lasted that long, she thought, seeing his hands clench tightly as though he was striving for control. 'J-just now you spoke about faith,' she stammered, and swallowed. 'Well, I couldn't marry you tomorrow without—telling you that I've br-broken faith with you.'

He was out of his chair and hauling her to her feet before the last word was spoken. And if she had thought him furious before, she saw he was livid with her now as he went out of control and violently shook her.

'You saw your ex-boy-friend when you were in London,' he raged accusingly. '*My God,* you *dared* to give him what's *mine!*' he shouted possessively.

'No, No,' she said quickly, terrified. Never had she thought to see him like this. '*No, Thorp,*' she cried hurriedly, seeing he was white about the mouth with fury. 'Nothing like that. I didn't mean that—didn't mean I'd broken faith that way.'

As though he didn't trust himself to hold her any longer, he thrust her away from him to the settee, uncaring of the way she bounced from the force of his thrust as he towered over her. 'Then you'd better tell me, and fast, which way you did mean,' he snarled, and she wasn't hesitating any longer. He'd scared the life out of her just then, his look had been one of pure murder.

'It's not that I don't want to marry you,' she explained, careless that she might be giving too much away in her need to placate him. 'But—but I don't think you'll want to marry me when I . . .' she paused, needing to see if any of his control had returned before she came to the part that could send the mercury of his temper skywards again.

'For God's sake spit it out,' he commanded, and for all his voice was rough, she was pleased to see he was looking more like the Thorp she thought she knew. 'If you haven't been giving yourself to someone else, what in the name of creation have you been up to?'

'I-I tricked you into asking me to marry you,' she confessed, not daring to look at him, the palms of her hands moist.

'You did?' he enquired slowly.

It was only a temporary respite, she knew; she couldn't hear any anger in his voice now. In actual fact, she thought, all her senses attuned to every nuance, he sounded as though he was confident she hadn't tricked him at all.

'And how did you do that, Jancy?' he asked as though intrigued. 'I clearly remember you telling me that the results of that night when we slept in the same bed were nil.'

'It—I . . .'

She was already struggling before she felt him come to sit down beside her. When his arm came casually along the back of the settee, her brain refused to function altogether. And it wasn't fear of him this time that was making a nonsense of her efforts to think straight. As always when he was this close, she was vitally aware of the sensual pleasure he gave her. He left his arm along the back of the settee and her brain patterns began sorting themselves out that that arm wasn't going to come around her shoulders.

'Oh, Thorp,' she said, pain in her voice, as some force outside herself had her turning to look at him. His look was encouraging, not angry. 'I couldn't marry you tomorrow knowing that—that I've lied to you from the very beginning. I didn't—you never . . .' Her heart pounding, she looked away. Then, taking a deep breath, she caught at a moment of strength and blurted out, 'That night we shared a bed—well,' her moment of strength was speeding away, 'well,' she took another breath, 'well, we didn't— that is—you never touched me.'

She tensed, waiting for the violence she had so recently witnessed in him to rise again, to break from the control he had on it as had happened not so many minutes ago. If he didn't physically attack her, then she didn't hold out much hope that she wouldn't feel the whiplash of his tongue.

But nothing was coming from him. Yet she dared not look at him again. And then, suddenly, she *was* looking at him, her mouth dropping in shock, her eyes wide and disbelieving. For he did speak. And what he said then was a shattering:

'I know,' he said calmly.

'*You know!*' she gasped, her green eyes showing her incredulity. 'But—how can you know? You can't. You were drunk. You passed . . .'

'Correction,' said Thorp, and it didn't do her the least

little bit of good that that arm left the back of the settee and settled lightly across her shoulders. '*You* thought I was drunk. But I was nowhere near to being witless.' Disbelievingly, she stared at him, her eyes widening further when he added, 'I can recall clearly everything that happened that night.'

'You can?' she croaked.

He nodded. 'That particular night I had been invited to give a talk in Todsbridge. Because of that, though you probably didn't notice, I drank nothing before or during dinner.'

Still too shaken to think of anything to say when he paused, she stayed quiet, the pink of never having fooled him for a minute flushing over her cheeks as he went on to let her know that the only one fooled, had been her.

'Though there was a glass of water at hand should I require it,' he continued, 'the evening turned out to be a very dry affair.' He broke off, his eyes taking in her heightened colour. And then, quietly, he dropped out the words, 'The only alcoholic drink I had that night, Jancis, was the one I poured when I came home.'

'But,' weakly she tried to argue, 'but you passed out on my bed. I saw your shoulders shake before you succumbed to the . . .'

Thorp shook his head, one corner of his mouth picking up. 'If you saw my shoulders shake it was most likely because I was having the damnedest job trying not to laugh out loud at the way you catapulted off the bed.'

'Laugh?' she echoed, astounded.

'You're going to have to forgive me, Jancy, but if you recall you'd called me a few most uncomplimentary names. I'm afraid your graphic description of the way you saw me aroused an urge in me to make you eat your words. So I came to your room with the sole intention of showing you that I did have moments when the term "strait-laced misery" couldn't be applied. I never intended to stay the night. A brief visit to confuse your opinion was all I had in mind—plus a few words of my own for the girl I then thought you were. But before I could grab hold of you you'd lit out from the room as though all the devils of hell were after you.'

'But—but you stayed in my bed,' she protested, hardly crediting that she could have been so wrong. 'You were still unconscious when I came back.'

'I was *asleep*,' Thorp amended, his fingers straying in stroking movements down her arm, in no way helping her to get her thoughts into any sort of order. 'Having experienced some of your temper, I was certain you'd be back to let go at me. So I lay there waiting. I closed my eyes savouring the one or two names I had ready for *you* when you did return. You were a long time, and quite simply, the weariness of a busy day got to me first—I fell asleep.'

Jancis exhaled one long breath. She should have taken notice when Sophie had told her about Thorp, she had warned her that just when you thought you had him neatly trussed up, he turned the tables and showed you all your knots were granny knots. She had made a complete and utter fool of herself. All this time—all the time she had been acting the seduced house guest, he had known he hadn't . . . She wished she could have felt angry then. Her colour was high, but not from temper. Vaguely something stirred in her mind that she had thought the next day that he hadn't been drunk, yet it was still hard to take in.

'You've known all the time,' she groped, 'that . . . From the moment you woke up and I accused you, you've known that I . . . that you never . . .'

'Never made love to you,' he finished for her, seeing the struggle she was having to complete even one sentence. 'Yes, I've known,' he said quietly, then added something that had her mind going in all directions, though at that moment she just didn't have the nerve to ask the meaning of. 'And it's been sheer hell,' he said mysteriously.

'Oh,' she said, not understanding. Then, making a tremendous effort to keep her mind on one track, 'Yet—yet you were still prepared to marry me?'

'I intend to marry you, Jancis,' he said, to her utmost relief, so that she just couldn't stay the smile that winged from the very heart of her as just at that moment Thorp turned her in his arm to look at her.

Her smile, though quickly cancelled, was observed by him, and it was his turn to take a deep breath as his other hand came up beneath her chin, forcing her to look at him. Then he was telling her something that had the room spinning about her for one dizzying moment.

'I intended to marry you, Jancis, from the moment I discovered I was in love with you.'

'In love with . . .' she said on a whisper of breath, while the room righted itself.

'You sound surprised,' Thorp said gently. 'I must have made a better cover-up than I thought.'

She'd had no idea, couldn't believe it. 'You were trying to hide it?' she gasped, not knowing why, how, or for that matter anything.

'I had to,' he said, drinking in the wonderment in her wonderful green eyes. 'I wasn't sure at first that you still weren't intending to make me pay for daring to think what I originally did about you.'

'You knew then why I—did what I did? You understand why I . . .'

'I pieced it together,' he told her, admitting ruefully, 'I probably deserved it since I'd been so rough on you— though in my defence you did let me get away with thinking you were—free and easy.'

'I was never like that,' said Jancis, wanting only his good opinion of her.

'I know that now,' said Thorp. 'I've known it for a long time.' He paused, looked at her, saw her trusting beautiful face, and couldn't resist her lips. Gathering her closely to him, he kissed her, and Jancis knew heaven after over a week of sheer hell.

But that heaven was only brief, for she felt his fingers digging into her arms as his mouth left hers and he pushed her gently away.

'I'm getting sidetracked,' he said, not looking nearly as controlled as he was sounding. 'As I was saying, I had to hide the way I feel about you because I didn't know that at the very last moment you wouldn't hit me for six by telling me it was all done for retribution and that you never did have any intention of marrying me.'

An audible gasp broke from her. 'I wouldn't do anything as terrible as that,' she protested in amazement. 'All the arrangements have been made. Paula's worked hard to . . .'

'In my sensible moments I didn't think you would either,' said Thorp. 'But since falling in love with you, my dear one,' the endearment thrilled, was added energy to her already fast pumping heart, 'I've known very few sensible moments. I've always been able to think logically, to analyse each problem I have come across. To take apart and piece together and satisfactorily document all my findings. I've always been able to catalogue everything I've done into correct compartments.' He smiled, a smile that had her bones melting. 'And then I fell in love, and it was goodbye to all that.'

Speechlessly Jancis could only stare at him. She had done that to him? Desperately she wanted to tell him she loved him, but couldn't, though she rather thought he knew.

'I've swung back and forth like a pendulum,' he told her. 'When you've been in my arms and seemed ready, like me, to forget everything else but the feeling that was so right between us, I've been overjoyed, only to fall into a dark pit of jealousy when I've thought of you with that ex-boy-friend you loved.'

'*Thought* I loved,' she said shyly, wondering anew that he had felt that same awful jealousy she had experienced over him and Aileen Forbes. She was pulled closely to him for her confession, while he told her:

'It was from remembering you saying that while you *thought*,' he smiled, 'you were in love with him, you still couldn't give way to the temptation to go to bed with him, that I received my greatest hope that you might love me.'

'Because you knew I didn't have to think about giving in when you kissed me?' she whispered, adding barely audibly, though Thorp heard it, 'You knew it was unconditional surrender the moment you held me in your arms?'

'Yes,' he said softly, and Jancis blushed. 'But even then I didn't trust the logic of my mind. I was too scared to tell you how I felt in case it was a game you were playing.' His look was serious as he revealed, 'It's been hell waiting for our wedding to be over tomorrow so that I could breathe one heartfelt sigh of relief before beginning to show you a little of what you mean to me.'

'Oh, Thorp,' she said in a choked voice. To think Thorp, who was always so sure of himself, must have been going through the same nightmarish time she had lived through!

'When I saw you at the door tonight, I felt like slamming it shut on you,' he confessed. 'I didn't want to hear anything you had to say. Well,' he corrected after a moment, 'not what I thought you'd come to say.' He looked at her steadily, then said in that even tone that only now she was beginning to realise meant he was trying for control, 'Though I wouldn't at all mind if you gave me some indication of how you feel about me.'

Her shyness fled as she discovered he really needed to know, he really needed to hear her say it. 'Don't you know?' she asked softly.

'I still don't trust the logic of my thinking,' he said, his voice controlled.

'Oh, Thorp,' she said, a great joy upon her, 'I love you so much it hurts!'

And that was all he waited to hear before his arms tightened and his mouth was meeting hers. As if drowning, Jancis clung to him. 'I love you,' she said again when he released her mouth to kiss her arched throat. 'I've been in torment thinking you didn't want to marry me.'

'Not want to marry you!' he muttered, letting her know there was no way she was going to do anything other. 'I've loved you and been determined to marry you ever since that night you saw me in town with Aileen Forbes and told me you couldn't marry me. You sounded so definite, and I was staggered to find that I wanted to marry you more than anything in the world.'

Jancis pulled back, looking deeply into his grey eyes. 'Was that when you found out you loved me?'

He nodded, his eyes warm on her face. 'I was shaken to the core,' he said. 'I can remember the feeling now. You sat there with your nose in the air, looking coldly arrogant, as though nothing on God's earth would make you change your mind. And the thought came from nowhere, "Oh, yes, she'd got to marry me—I'm in love with her".'

She was having a hard time catching her breath at the look of adoration he was giving her. 'Oh, Thorp,' she whispered, 'and it was that very same day I realised I was in love with you. I'd seen you with Aileen Forbes and I've never felt so violently ill in my life. I never want to experience jealousy like that again.'

'You won't have to, my darling,' he told her tenderly. 'Just remember I love you so completely, there's no room in my heart for anyone but you.'

She reached to him and kissed him, then found it was Thorp who was doing the kissing. But this time it was she who broke from him. They still had some talking to do, yet if he kissed her once more like that, she knew anything she wanted to ask him would soon be forgotten.

'Thorp,' she said, puzzled, when with a reluctance that thrilled her he let her lips do something other than return his kisses, 'you'd asked me to marry you before that night. Were you playing with me then or . . .' Her voice tapered off as she recalled that up until that day, as far as she was concerned, for her it had all been so much a way of getting even with him.

'Had you any intention of going through with it until then?' he countered. And when she had the grace to blush, he laughed softly. 'I thought not,' he said. 'That's why I told Sophie we were engaged. I thought it would be interesting to see what you'd do next.'

'You beast!' she smiled, knowing he had cornered her neatly, but she couldn't help laughing too. She reckoned she had deserved to be made to wriggle after telling that terrible lie in the first place.

'Though,' he admitted with a self-deprecating grin, 'if it's any consolation, I don't think I ever was immune to you.'

'You weren't?' Jancis put in, eager to learn more.

'Apart from the unreasonable amount of disgust I felt at that party when I saw the way the beautiful, honest child I remembered had turned out, I think I must have known as far back as that day in your flat when Sophie was pulling her Dying Swan act and suggesting you came with us to look after her, that I was making a bachelor's last stand against the inevitable. Even so, when I could so easily have scuppered her plans by reminding her what she'd so conveniently forgotten, that Mrs Hemmings is a trained nurse, I found that instead of reminding her, I was challenging you to come with us. I realise now that it was because I wanted you in my home—wanted you where I could see you every day.'

Her eyes were shining with happiness. 'You didn't mean it, then, that business about wanting to marry me because you wanted an heir?' she teased, glorying that she could now be so free with him.

'That will be a bonus,' he said, then, his face serious, 'For the moment the only thing I want is to be able to put that gold ring on your wedding finger tomorrow.'

It seemed natural that they should kiss again. But after having had a week of torment, Jancis still had some questions and was in heaven that she didn't have to hold back any more.

'Why,' she asked, puzzlement threaded in her voice once more, 'why, Thorp, did you tell Aileen Forbes you wouldn't be seeing her again? You weren't seriously considering marrying me at that time.'

'It seemed to me that since I'd told Sophie you and I were engaged I couldn't in all fairness do anything other,' he said, then added, to her delight, 'We were about to wind up anyway.'

Her smile peeped out once more. 'Am I asking too many questions?' she asked, though for the life of her she couldn't help it.

'If by answering your questions I'm able to clear away any doubts you may have, however small, then ask away, my darling,' Thorp answered her.

But by that time Jancis didn't have any doubts at all. Thorp loved her; as unbelievable as it seemed, he loved her. It was there in his face, in the way he held her. And tomorrow she would be his wife. A cover of pure bliss enveloped her, and for countless moments she just looked back at him. Then she recalled something he had said very much earlier, and again she found a question to ask him.

'When you said you knew that we had never—hadn't— well, you know,' she stammered, feeling her colour rising, discovering suddenly there was still a long way to go before she could feel entirely at ease on the subject with him. 'Well, you said then that knowing was sheer hell. What . . .?'

'What did I mean?' said Thorp, and then went on to enlighten her. 'According to you we'd been lovers. I had to pretend I believed that. But,' and here he gave her such a warm look, it had her anticipating his next statement, 'there were many times when I had to hold back the urge for that not to become a fact. Not least the occasion of the night before I went to India. How I wanted you that night! Even now I don't know from where I found the will power to leave you.'

'But why did you leave?' flew from her before she could check it, and her cheeks went scarlet for all she knew he was aware she wouldn't have been able to stop herself from giving herself to him that night.

'Because, my dear, sweet innocent Jancy, had I given way to the urges that were interfering with my thinking, then you would have given me proof that no one had touched you before—and that included me.'

'Oh,' she said, colouring. Of course. Thorp was an experienced man; he would have known she was still a virgin. 'Oh,' she said again. 'And as soon as I realised that you knew . . .'

'That very frail thread by which our engagement hung would be broken. And since I didn't want you to find the smallest reason for backing out of marrying me, I've had to go through hell each time I've seen you, wanting to take you in my arms but too scared to do so in case my will power wasn't up to letting you go when things started getting out of hand—as I knew they would.'

'You wanted to marry me that badly?' she breathed softly on a whisper.

'It was all I could think about. I've been in hell,' he told her, 'knowing that some time you were going to come clean about that night. Scared stiff to phone you when

I've been longing to hear your voice in case you would tell me not only that, but that our wedding was off. I thought if we could get past the ceremony, then when we were on our own tomorrow your conscience would have you telling me. And then you arrived at my door tonight, and everything went out of my head but the thought of Oh, no, she's come to call it off.'

'Oh, darling,' Jancis whispered, shattered that they had both spent agonising hours. 'I want to marry you so much, I shall probably be at the church before you tomorrow!'

'I doubt it,' Thorp said convincingly, then she was in his arms once more, and this time there was no need for restraint from either side.

The settee was wide and deep and its full length was made use of as Thorp moved with her until she was lying with him, their two bodies pressed closely together.

'I love you, I love you, I love you,' he whispered tenderly, kissing her eyes, trailing kisses down the side of her face, his lips fixing hungrily on her parted mouth, his passion blotting out all thought save this was where she belonged.

'Thorp—darling,' she sighed against his mouth, thrilling to his touch as the buttons on her shirt became no hindrance to his need to feel her warm silken body beneath his hands.

Again they kissed, and as he pressed her deeper into the cushions moving his body until he was lying over her, her fingers explored his chest, found buttons, and like him she wanted to feel the warmth of his skin. The feel of the rough hair on his chest delighted her and he groaned at the feel of her at first tentatively exploring fingers.

'I love you, Thorp,' she uttered ecstatically when he raised his head to look deeply into her luminous green eyes. She felt the lower half of his hard body press further to her. 'Oh, darling,' she moaned, her need for him swamping her.

'I want you, my lovely Jancy,' he said deep in his throat, his grey eyes hot for her, his skin flushed. And as she arched to press herself yet bruisingly closer to him, any remaining control he had left him, 'Oh, my darling, I've got to have you. I can't,' a shudder shook him, 'I can't wait. Please don't ask me to wait.'

'Will you take me to your bed?' she asked, her voice husky, shy, in spite of her question.

'My woman,' he said, his voice fiercely possessive, every thread of sound telling her she was his and heaven help anyone who thought differently.

She was in his arms, being carried across the hall, when the telephone shrilled in a ghastly shriek of sound that had no place in the world they were in. Startled, they looked at each other and Jancis knew when Thorp strode straight past the telephone table that he meant to ignore it.

'It might be Sophie,' she said, coming to the surface of the rapturous land Thorp had taken her to. 'She was worried about me when I left the house.'

'Oh, no!' Thorp groaned, clearly in two minds whether or not to let his niece stay worried. Then suddenly something seemed to occur to him, and carrying her to the phone table he set her down and still keeping one arm tight about her, picked up the phone.

It was Sophie. She heard Thorp reassuring her that she was fine. She didn't know at all what Sophie was saying after that, but she felt surging disappointment sweep through her when after some moments of listening, he looked at her, his expression rueful as he said down the mouthpiece:

'I'm bringing Jancy back now.' Mutely, trying to hide her disappointment, she looked at him, and Thorp leaned down to place a gentle kiss on her mouth before, as though having to drag his attention back to the phone, he instructed Sophie to, 'Put her on.' He then handed the phone to Jancis. 'Someone wants to speak to you, darling,' he said softly.

'Hello,' said Jancis, more conscious that Thorp's arm had gone from her to allow her to concentrate than of the voice on the other end of the phone. Then she recognised the voice, and tears came to her eyes.

Her eyes were still shimmering when she replaced the phone some minutes later. 'That was my mother!' she said.

'I know,' said Thorp, smiling, and suddenly she knew that he had done this for her.

'You arranged it, didn't you?' she asked, feeling tearful again that here was another way in which he was showing his love for her.

'I thought you wanted her to be there tomorrow.'

'Oh, I did,' she said, swallowing hard to hold back the tears. 'But how did you . . .'

'Sophie told me you'd tried to contact her but that she was in St Moritz. I knew Barney Tavistock wasn't short of a few coppers, so I thought if they were staying in a hotel it would be the best. I managed to get in touch with your mother after a few abortive attempts, and she said nothing would keep her away from seeing you married. Sophie tells me she arrived about ten minutes after you'd left.'

'Darling Thorp,' said Jancis, her eyes aglow. 'Thank you. Thank you so very much!'

'You can say thank you better than that, can't you?' he teased. And the next moment she was in his arms, and it was as though she had never left them. Until, when she thought that soon he would carry her upstairs, Thorp suddenly broke from her, his breathing fractured.

'You meant it when you said you were taking me back to Little Bramington, didn't you?' she asked, her own breathing not very steady.

His hands dropped to his sides and he took a step away

from her as though not fully trusting himself. 'I'm afraid
so, sweetheart. Your mother will be waiting up to say
hello to you.'

'Yes, yes, of course,' she said, her voice flat, as she tried
for a brave smile. For much as she was looking forward to
seeing her mother, she was still on that high plateau that
Thorp's lovemaking had taken her to, and her emotions
were chaotic at being left stranded up there; it hurt.

'I want you, my darling, make no mistake about that,'
he told her, lest she should think for one second there was
any doubt about it. 'But not in a hurried fashion, because
we know the lights in that house in Little Bramington are
all on waiting for you. When we come together—after
that first time, that first time for you—well, it might not
be all you imagined it might be.'

Her heart winged out to him. Dear, wonderful Thorp!
He was telling her in the plainest way possible that he
wasn't rejecting her, if that was what her hurt look had
said, trying to tell her that in that first time there might
be pain for her, but, shy suddenly again, she couldn't
answer him.

'Understand, my darling,' he said tenderly, 'I want you
now so much that it's agony to deny my need for you. But
I don't want any hurried meeting. I want time to break
down any last-minute reservations you're not now aware
of, but which may be there. I want time after our love
has been consummated to soothe away any distress you
may feel. I want to spend the night cradling you in my
arms. I want to show you I love you with every part of
me, not just my body. To let you know that that will be
the only time I will ever knowingly cause you pain.'

Her eyes misted over. To have someone loving her like
this, to love her so much he would deny himself to ensure
her happiness, was all so new to her it would take some
getting used to.

'Thorp Kingman,' she said, her love for him shining

from her eyes, 'I think you're the most wonderful man I've ever known.' Then striving with all she knew for a teasing note, because their emotions charged, Thorp too must be under a terrific strain, 'I'll meet you in church tomorrow,' she said. 'And just in case you don't recognise me, I'll be the one walking down the aisle on the arm of your brother-in-law.'

He laughed as she hoped he would. 'Come on, sweetheart, let's get your coat. You can leave your car, it will save having to pick it up when we come back from our honeymoon.'

Honeymoon—what a beautiful word that was! This time tomorrow she would again be alone with Thorp, only then, she would be cradled in his arms.

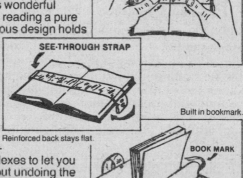